NO OTHER LIFE

NAN A. TALESE

DOUBLEDAY
NEW YORK
LONDON
TORONTO
SYDNEY
AUCKLAND

BRIAN
MOORE

NO

———

OTHER

———

LIFE

PUBLISHED BY NAN A. TALESE
an imprint of Doubleday
a division of Bantam Doubleday Dell Publishing Group, Inc.
1540 Broadway, New York, New York 10036

All of the characters in this book are fictitious,
and any resemblance to actual persons, living or
dead, is purely coincidental.

Book design by Paul Randall Mize

Library of Congress Cataloging-in-Publication Data

Moore, Brian, 1921–
No other life/Brian Moore.—1st ed. in the U.S.A.
p.   cm.
I. Title.
PR9199.3.M617N6   1993
813'.54—dc20   92-41181
CIP

ISBN 0-385-41515-X

Printed in the United States of America
September 1993
First Edition in the United States of America

1   3   5   7   9   10   8   6   4   2

For Jean

God moves the player, he, in turn, the piece. But what god beyond God begins the round of dust and time and dream and agonies?

—JORGE LUIS BORGES

NO OTHER LIFE

ONE

IN THE OLD DAYS they would have given me a gold watch. I never understood why. Was it to remind the one who is being retired that his time is past? Instead of a watch I have been presented with a videotape of the ceremonies. My life here has ended. My day is done.

Next week I will leave Ganae and fly to a retreat house in Cuba. I have never lived in Cuba. Canada, where I was born and bred, is only a memory. You might ask why I was not permitted to end my days here. I am one of the last white priests on this island and the last foreign principal of the Collège St Jean. At the ceremonies on Tuesday night, this was not mentioned. But yesterday, alone in the sitting room of our residence, watching the videotape which they have made for me, I saw myself as they must now see me. The ceremony was held in the college auditorium. Priests, nuns, students and dignitaries, all were mulatto or black. On the wall behind the microphones and the podium there was a large photograph of our new Pope, himself a man of mixed blood. And then, walking towards the podium, a ghost from the past, this stooped white man in a frayed cassock, incongruous as the blackamoor attendant in a sixteenth-century painting of the

French court. I am a reminder of a past they feel is best forgotten. They are happy to see me go.

And yet, on the videotape, they weep, they embrace me. Some profess love for me. One of my former students, now the Minister for Foreign Affairs, praised me in his address for my efforts to bring the benefits of higher education to scholarship students from city slums and rural backwaters. There was applause when he said it, but how many in his audience thought of Jeannot at that moment? Jeannot, the most important milestone of my life, is nowhere mentioned in this farewell ceremony. On the video screen, surrounded by smiling faces, I cut slices from a large cake. The videotape, like the gold watch of other days, attests that I lived and worked with these people for most of my adult life. It is a memento.

But what sort of memento? I am a member of the Albanesians, a Catholic teaching Order, founded in France. Unlike lay people who retire, I have no family, no children, or grandchildren, no link with normal life. My brother and my sister are strangers I have not seen for many years. When a religious retires it is as though he is struck down with a fatal illness. His earthly task is over. Now he must prepare himself for death. In another age it was a time of serenity, of waiting to be joined with God and those who have gone before. But, for me, death is a mystery, the answer to that question which has consumed my life.

At the ceremonies last Tuesday, our boys' choir sang the school song. The words were composed by Father Ricard, a French priest who was principal here before my time. It is a sort of hymn in which God is asked to bless our school and, through education, to bring wealth and happiness to Ganae and its people. Father Pinget makes mock of this song saying that, evidently, God does not speak French.

French, of course, is out of favour now. When I came here it was the opposite. Creole was the language of the poor. To speak French was to show that one belonged, or aspired to belong, to the mulatto elite. Now, Creole is the official tongue. But does God speak Creole?

I think of these things because I am looking at the empty pages of my life. My years here have counted for little. I have failed in most of the things that I set out to do. But I am a man with a secret, with a story never told. Even now, as I write it down, is it the moment to tell the truth?

Where should I begin? Shall I begin with the anxiety that came upon me last night as I removed from the walls of my room the photograph of my parents and a second photograph showing my graduating class, long ago, at the University of Montreal? I put them in the trunk that contains my belongings, the same flat tin trunk which was carried up to this room when I first arrived in Ganae, thirty years ago. Next week, when they carry that trunk downstairs, there will be no sign that I ever lived here. I think it is that—the knowledge that the truth of these events may never be known—that makes me want to leave this record.

But how should I tell it? When we are young we assume that, in age, we will be able to look back and remember our lives. But just as we forget the details of a story a few months after hearing it, so do the years hang like old clothes, forgotten in the wardrobe of our minds. Did I wear that? Who was I then?

That is a question I cannot answer. I can tell you that my name is Paul Michel and that I was born sixty-five years ago in the town of Ville de la Baie in Northern Quebec. My father was a doctor in that town and when he died my younger brother, Henri, took over the practice. Why did *I* not become a doctor? I do not remember that, as a child, I was especially devout. I was educated by the Albanesian Fathers at their college in Montreal and when I showed some glimmerings of literary talent the Order offered me a chance to do graduate work at McGill University and, later, sent me for a year to read French literature at the Sorbonne. Now, looking back, I do not know if I had a true vocation for the priesthood. I was attracted to the Order by its propaganda about devoting one's life to teaching the poor in faraway places. I became an Albanesian Father much as others of my generation were to join the Peace Corps.

The priesthood meant celibacy and that, for me, caused a terrible confusion. I would feel hopeless longings for a girl seen in the street, followed by a depression which my prayers could not cure. In Paris, I fell in love. She was a fellow student at the Sorbonne. On her part, it was innocent. I was just a friend. I thought for a time of giving up the priesthood and asking her . . . but I did nothing. It was not until I was posted to Ganae that my longing for her was eased. Here, far from any world I had known, I would live my life as God's servant, doing His work.

I was soon disappointed. I had come to teach the poor. Ganae is in the Caribbean, but is as poor as any African country. Eighty per cent of the population is illiterate. The few state schools are pathetically inefficient. The state university is an inferior training college which turns out substandard doctors and engineers. Our school, the Collège St Jean in Port Riche, is the only private institution of higher education. It was founded to produce students who could gain admission to foreign universities when they completed their high-school studies and went abroad. For this reason it was, from the beginning, a school for the sons of the mulatto elite, an elite who lived in large estates behind high walls and security gates, waited on by black servants, an elite who aped French manners, served champagne and *haute cuisine*, and gossiped about the new couture collections and the latest Parisian *scandale*. When I began to teach at the Collège St Jean, we had fewer than twenty black students in our classrooms.

Why was this so? Our Principal, Father Bourque, explained it this way. 'The mulattos run Ganae, they always have. They control the parliament, they have business ties with the US and France. By educating their children we have a chance to influence events. This is a black republic but the shade of black is all important. Light skins rule. When a *noir* becomes successful he tries to marry into the *mulâtre* class. Besides, our Archbishop is a conservative. He wants to maintain the status quo.'

What would I have done if things had not held out some hope of change? Would I have become disillusioned and pragmatic like Father Bourque? Luckily, I was not put to the test. A few months after my arrival, in one of those political shifts not unknown in Ganae, a black country dentist named Jean-Marie Doumergue ran for election, promising to abolish torture, promote democracy, and curb the powers of the police. The Army saw in Doumergue a puppet they could use to control the black masses. Doumergue was elected. But, at once, he began to attack the privileges of the mulatto elite.

Why do we remember certain mornings, certain meetings? I can still recall my anxiety on that morning when I stood outside our Principal's office with eight black boys clustered around me. The Archbishop had just arrived. Our Principal opened his office door and beckoned me to bring the boys inside. I bowed humbly to Archbishop Le Moyne, a cold Breton whom I did not know. He and the Principal went on talking as though the boys were not in the room.

'We are dealing with a new situation,' Father Bourque said. 'We now have a president who repeats constantly that he has a mandate to improve the education of his fellow *noirs*, a president who complains about schools like ours. There are no other schools like ours. He is talking about our school. And so, Your Grace, if you will bear with me, I would like to propose that we increase the number of our scholarship pupils immediately. I am thinking of a sizeable number of scholarships. Perhaps forty. And they should all be *noirs*.'

But the Archbishop did not agree. 'I'm afraid the elite will not tolerate their children mixing with children of the slums.

A few more *noirs*, yes. The elite does not wish to seem big-oted, especially with a *noir* in power. But forty black students —where would you find them?'

Our Principal turned to me. 'Father Michel has been doing some groundwork in that regard. Father?'

I was holding a sheaf of test results. I was, as always in those days, nervous and overanxious. 'Your Grace,' I said, 'I have been travelling around the rural districts, and, believe me, I have had no trouble finding *noir* children of higher than average intelligence. Here are eight of them. For example, this little fellow seems quite exceptional. And yet he is an orphan, from the poorest of the poor—the village of Toumalie, if that means anything to Your Grace?'

As I was speaking I kept an eye on the boys. The other seven stood humbly, like animals whose sale was in the bal-ance. But the one I had singled out, the boy named Jeannot, stared at us as though he, not we, were deciding his future. And then, suddenly, this boy said, 'I wish to be a priest, Your Grace. No one from Toumalie has ever been a priest.'

Afterwards, at lunch, the Archbishop asked, 'Surely you are not planning to make priests out of these little *noirs*? The college is not a seminary.'

Our Principal laughed. 'The boy from Toumalie? I don't know why he said that. Probably to make us take him in. Do you know, Paul?'

I suppose Father Bourque was merely trying to bring me into the conversation. I had sat tongue-tied throughout the meal. But, because I desperately wanted to have the boys ac-cepted by the school, I answered with an evasion.

'I have no idea,' I said. 'I hardly know the boy.'

It was true, yet not true. By then, I was much involved with Jeannot although I had met him only two weeks before, while combing the few rural schools in the north of the island. A teacher in the village of Toumalie took me to his tin-roofed schoolhouse, excitedly talking of a thirteen-year-old boy, an

orphan who, he said, 'is a vessel into which you can put anything and bring it back out again.' I tested the boy. I was
astonished. The following day I rode on muleback over a
road never travelled by motor vehicles, up to a mud-walled
mountain shack on land denuded by three hundred years of
ignorant and relentless agriculture. There, a woman with the
flayed face and wasted body of those who live on the rim of
starvation sat on a ramshackle porch, breast-feeding a child.
She was a widow with four children of her own and two boys
who were the orphaned children of her brother, a warehouse
clerk who had died three years ago. One of these orphans was
the boy, Jean-Paul Cantave, known as Jeannot. When I told
her my plan she gave him into my care as casually as she
would give away a puppy from a litter.

An hour later I rode back down the mountainside, the boy
hanging on behind me, his arms around my waist as the mule
picked its way over the rutted road. He was small and frail.
His clothes were a dirty denim shirt, patched trousers and
wooden-soled clogs. Imagine—no papers, no signature, no
document of any kind. What would I do with him if the
Archbishop refused to accept him? He had been given to me.
I wondered if people back in Canada had any idea of what life
was like here. No one in the world had any idea. This was
Ganae.

The other children I had selected were not orphans and so
remained at home until the day, two weeks later, when we
brought them before the Archbishop. But Jeannot I took
straight back to the college, where I installed him in a dormi-
tory with ten other boarders, all of them mulattos. After the
first night he came to me. 'They are laughing at me because
they have clothes to go to bed in. I do not.'

He did not speak to me as a teenaged boy might speak to a
person in authority. From the beginning, it was as though we
were friends. I went out at once and bought pyjamas and
underclothes. And, although he had not yet been accepted in

the school, I arranged for him to be provided with the school uniform. In the next several days he learned to eat in the same manner as the rich boys, to blow his nose in a handkerchief, to take a daily shower and, above all, to use French as his first language. Until then it was the tongue he had learned in school, but now, surrounded by boys who spoke it in preference to Creole, he became fluent with astonishing speed. In fact, when two weeks later the other black scholarship students showed up, Jeannot was no longer of their world. The village teacher in Toumalie was right. He was a vessel into which you could put anything and bring it back out again.

He had been given to me. Almost every day when his classes ended he would leave the college and walk six streets to the staff residence where I lived. Hyppolite would admit him and he would sit on a stool in the corridor, reading and studying, but waiting to see if I would go with him for a walk. Yes, like a dog. I often thought of that. But I cannot say that he was devoted to me. He watched me, he studied me, he tried to find out how my mind worked. From the time he came into my care he completely cut himself off from his former life. When I asked if he had written to his brother and cousins, he said, 'What use would it be to write? They will forget me. All that is over, isn't it, Father? Now, I live in the city. I would never have seen the city if you had not taken me from Toumalie. You will not be sorry. I will do well for you. I am your boy.'

It was true. The other masters, seeing him waiting for me in the halls of the residence, began to refer to him as 'Paul's boy.' And when Christmas came around and the college closed down for the holidays what were we to do with Jeannot? I spoke to Father Bourque. 'Let him stay at our residence,' he said. 'He can sleep in the basement with Hyppolite. Why send him back to people who have given him away?'

On that holiday because I was new to Ganae Jeannot and I

discovered the city together. We went by bus into the hills of Bellevue to look at the splendid estates of the elite. We walked down the deserted ceremonial avenues of the Bicentennial Exposition Grounds, peering in at abandoned showrooms, built in the fifties when the government foolishly tried to ape the expansionist schemes of other, more prosperous, lands. We visited the national casino on the seafront and watched Swiss croupiers, elegant in white dinner jackets, spin roulette wheels and deal baccarat for American tourists, ashore for the day from the cruise ships which then called at Port Riche. Together, we roamed the cluttered aisles of the city's open-air market and crossed the Place de la République to peer through gilded railings at the gleaming white bulk of the presidential palace. On Christmas morning we attended Mass in the Cathedral of Notre Dame de Secours and heard the choir sing Mass in Latin, a language Jeannot was beginning to learn. And then, on the day after Christmas, I took him to La Rotonde.

La Rotonde is a city within a city, the black swollen heart of Port Riche. It lies along the edge of the docks, hidden away from the tourist shops, the markets and the legislative buildings that border on the palace. It is a vast, fetid hive of narrow, mud-clotted lanes, stinking of open sewage, a warren of plywood and cardboard shacks, roofed with rotting tin, a place without electric light or running water, where naked children bathe in muddy puddles left over from last night's rains. Behind its filthy shanties, young girls, some of them no more than twelve years old, offer themselves to any passing man for fifty centos or, if he haggles, for less. Everything is for sale here. Cast-off clothing donated by American charities to the Ganaen Red Cross ends up on the street stalls of La Rotonde. Even human misery is put up for rent. If you walk deep enough into the maze of its narrow passageways, you will come suddenly into the sunlight of a central square, the Place Napoléon, where cripples, dwarfs, people covered with ugly sores, deformed children, women breast-feeding starveling babies, congregate each morning waiting to be paired off, a crippled man with a deformed child, a woman covered in sores with one of the famine babies, a dwarf with a blind girl. Deals are made, tableaux of human misery are assembled. Towards noon, a procession of these people moves out from La Rotonde going to the gift shops, the market and the port, to sit all afternoon in the unrelenting sun, waiting for some tourist from the cruise ships to drop a coin in their outstretched palms.

Why did I bring Jeannot to La Rotonde? Even in the desperate rural poverty of Toumalie he had never seen such sights. And why, again and again, did he insist that we return there? Were those walks responsible for what happened to him in later life when, from that same great slum, he began his journey towards fame?

In the months that followed Christmas, Jeannot was not the only scholarship boy who did brilliantly in class. The other seven were all above average and for a time there was talk of increasing their number to forty, as we had first envisaged. Doumergue, the new president, was still promising to fight illiteracy and provide proper schools for the poor. He was meek and soft-spoken; his reign seemed mild. At official audiences in the presidential palace, he wore an ill-fitting black suit and carried a battered Homburg hat which, when he sat on the thronelike presidential chair, he would hand apologetically to a bemedalled military aide who stood directly behind him. In all of his addresses he made a point of speaking in Creole, which displeased the elite. 'I am the president of all the people,' he said. 'I am *noir* and humble. I am the living incarnation of the people's wish to better their lives.'

Did we believe him? I wanted to. I hoped we were at the beginning of a new era. I pleaded with Father Bourque to speak to the Archbishop about taking in more *noirs*. But the

Archbishop informed us that no new scholarship students were to be accepted. 'Frankly,' he told our Principal, 'nothing has changed and nothing will change. Doumergue is a puppet. As always, the Army remains in charge.'

The Archbishop was wrong. As I was wrong. Things did change. But, in Ganae, bad news comes through rumour, whispers, night visits, soldiers shooting wildly in the streets. At the college we lived in a world apart, remote as the elite on their Bellevue estates. The arrests, the tortures, the clubbing of those few who dared to demonstrate, none of these things was reported in the newspapers. Radio, the all-important source of information in an illiterate country, remained majestically silent. Parliamentary debates were listened to by other politicians, but never by the people. Within a year of his election Doumergue was a dictator. But we didn't know it. It was, to my surprise, Jeannot, who first told me of the rumours of repression. I asked where he had heard them and he answered, 'Claude Lamballe.'

Claude Lamballe was one of Jeannot's classmates. His father, Simon, was a colonel in the Army and an instructor at the elite Académie Militaire. This same Simon Lamballe had, coincidentally, attended the Sorbonne in the period when I studied there. We did not know each other in Paris but when I met him at a school reception in Ganae, we became friendly because of our shared experience. And so, as no one at the college seemed to know the truth about Doumergue, I went one evening to Simon's Bellevue mansion.

'These rumours?' Simon said. 'All true.'

'But isn't it a fact that his election was backed by the Army? We've always assumed he's your creature.'

'He was,' Simon said. 'But now the Army is Dr Frankenstein.'

'Yet, he seems sincere.'

'Perhaps he was, once. I don't know him personally. But the history of Ganae is like a cheap gramophone record. The new tune plays for a while, then the needle sticks in the groove and the player-arm slumps back and slips off the disc. Every Ganaen leader begins his term by promising to change things. Most of them don't even try. But the few who do—well, it's like the gramophone record. The needle sticks in a groove. There are many grooves—the elite, the Army, foreign business interests, the people's illiteracy—you name it—there's no way that progress or democratic ideals can work here. And so the leader becomes a strong man, trying to force his ideas through. Enemies have to be disposed of. Coups must be anticipated and crushed. The leader becomes a tyrant. Doumergue is simply a victim of this country's history.'

'Can't the Army get rid of him?'

'Father, let me give you a little advice. You are a priest, and a white foreigner. But you may not ask such questions of me, or of anyone. When you are discussing Uncle D. you're not safe, no matter who you're talking to.'

Some weeks after this conversation I was visiting a former pupil who lived in the Laramie section of the city. As I left my pupil's house and walked up a side street which led to the Boulevard Carnot, four large *noirs* wearing blue seersucker overalls and carrying old-fashioned Lee-Enfield rifles came towards me. When they drew level, one of them stopped me by laying the barrel of his rifle across my chest. 'Cigarette, *Mon Pe*?'

I said I was sorry but I did not smoke.

'We do,' one of the men said. 'So we need money for cigarettes. Be quick now.'

They did not look like beggars. They had guns, after all. 'Who are you?' I said.

One of the men said to the others, 'Who are we? Why does he not know? He is a priest, not a tourist. He's making fun of us.'

'Don't make fun of us,' one of the others said.

'I have never hit a white face,' a third said. 'Maybe today is my day to hit a white face.'

'Give us money, quick,' the first man said. 'Ten pesons, OK?'

'I am a priest,' I said. 'Would you rob a priest?'

When I said that, the first man hit me with his closed fist. My nose dribbled blood. The second man swung the stock of his rifle and hit me on the shins. I stumbled and fell to my knees. They formed a circle around me. 'Ten pesons,' the first man said. 'Give it, or we will take it.'

Kneeling, blood dribbling into my mouth, I took out my purse and gave them a ten-peson note. For a moment I thought that they would take the rest of my money, but they did not. The first one took the note, held it up to the light, then put it in his pocket and nodded to the others. They walked away as though I did not exist.

When they were no longer in sight I stood up, my shins aching as I groped for a tissue to stem my nosebleed. Across the narrow street, a young girl was watching me from a second-storey window, but when I looked up at her she at once withdrew her head and closed the shutters. I fingered my nose. It was very painful. It could be broken. Behind me, I heard the sound of wooden clogs on the cobblestones. A tall woman from the countryside came up the empty street, carrying a large bundle of washing on her head. When she drew level she stopped and turned towards me, holding her head high to balance her load. *'Eh, ben, Mon Pe.* Bad times begin. You all right?'

'Who were they?'

She looked at me, eyes wide, as though she could not believe the question. 'You joking me?'

'No, no.'

'Bleus. They the bosses now. You didn't know?'

'No.'

She laughed, the huge load wobbling on her head. 'Where you been, *Mon Pe*?'

My nose was not broken but swollen in such a way that everyone in the college soon knew about the attack. On the streets of Port Riche the number of men wearing blue seersucker overalls and carrying old Lee-Enfield rifles increased until they became as common a sight as police and soldiers. And when Jeannot and I passed the presidential palace on one of our walks we saw, inside the gates, not only the ceremonial guards provided by the Army, but men in blue overalls, sitting in comfortable armchairs near the sentry boxes, their weapons at their feet. At night, trucks could be heard racing through the streets. Volleys of rifle fire woke us from our sleep. Then, on the third anniversary of his inauguration, Doumergue announced that he was closing down the Académie Militaire. I went to see my friend Simon Lamballe.

'It's all over,' he said. 'I've lost my job. I've been "promoted" to the Northern Command. The Académie is finished.'

'But why doesn't the Army do something?'

'Do what? It turns out that Uncle D. is a better student of history than the rest of us. He's found a formula. Tell the *noirs* you're their president and the enemy of the elite. Leave the rich alone to do what they've always done. In turn, they're grateful for being spared and so they render unto Caesar. As for the Army we thought his game would be to cause divisions by promoting *noirs* over us *mulâtres*. He's done something else. He's created his own army. The *bleus*.'

'So what will the Army do?'

Lamballe laughed. 'I could ask you the same thing. What will the Church do? Uncle wants black bishops. Ganaens. You foreigners will be pushed out.'

When I mentioned Lamballe's prophecy to the other professors, no one believed it. The Ganaen hierarchy had always been French. The people were religious and devoted to the

Pope. The attack on me by Doumergue's *bleus* was, everyone said, an aberration, the random violence of hired thugs.

A few weeks later while we were having supper in the refectory of the residence, two men wearing white suits and panama hats came in from the front hall and walked over to the refectory table. Our Principal rose up, irritated at this intrusion.

'Who are you? What are you doing here?'

The men ignored the question. One of them looked at the food on our plates. It was a supper of beans and rice. The man put his finger into the serving dish and stirred it around. 'What, no pork?' he said. 'Why do you eat like peasants, Reverend Fathers?'

'Because we are poor,' the Principal said. 'Now, who are you and what do you want?'

'Anti-terrorist Squad. Are you Father Bourque?'

'I am.'

'We want to talk to you. Do you have an office?'

When the Principal had gone off with the men, Father Noël Destouts, a Ganaen, said to me, 'I don't think they're police. They behave like *bleus*.'

The Principal did not return to finish his supper. After the meal we went, as usual, into the lounge where Hyppolite served coffee. As I took my cup from the tray I saw our Principal come downstairs with the two men. He led them to the front door and let them out. Then he came into the lounge. 'Paul? Will you come with me?'

The others looked at me in surprise. When I went upstairs with Father Bourque he did not speak until he had shut us into the privacy of his study. He went to his desk and took up a printed sheet of paper. 'This is a leaflet which those men brought here tonight. They say several copies of it were distributed in the Bellevue and Beaulieu districts two nights ago. They were handed out by some boys who, the police say, may be from our school.'

I read the leaflet. I don't remember the wording, but it said that Ganae was a dictatorship and the only way to free its people was by revolution which must be led by young people ready to give up their lives for the poor. I realised it could be a twisted version of something I had said in class a few weeks before. I had told my students that nothing would change in Ganae until educated young people like them were prepared to sacrifice their comfortable lives and prospects for the good of the poor.

'Well, Paul,' Father Bourque said. 'Do you know anything about this?'

'No . . . but . . .'

'But what?'

'Perhaps,' I said, stumbling with the words, 'it could have had something to do with a remark I made in class.'

'That's why I asked. I've been meaning to speak to you. I know your feelings about this country. But political comments in front of the boys are totally uncalled for. You're a priest, not a politician. We've got to be very careful. We're white people in a black country. Foreigners—never forget that. Tell me. Do you know anything about these leaflets?'

'No, Father. Why do the police say the boys could be from our school?'

'Apparently, they arrested fifteen poor souls who had accepted the leaflets. They took those people to Fort Noël and you can imagine what they did to them. These people told the police that the boys were well dressed, six mulattos and one black. All dressed like children of the elite.'

One black. I felt my heart in my chest.

'Anyway,' Father Bourque said. 'See what you can find out. And, in the meantime, let's not mention this to the rest of the staff.'

That night I lay awake. I thought of the policeman in his white suit putting his finger into the bowl that contained our food. I thought of those people arrested and now held in Fort

Noël, a place of torture, a place where protesters are silenced and disappear. When at last I slept, men in white suits stood over me, shouting, 'You are white people in a black country. Foreigners—never forget that.' I woke to the sounds of dawn in Port Riche. Roosters crowed. Food vendors, arriving from villages outside the city, passed below my window, the creaking of their ancient carts loud on the cobblestones. A church bell rang. I rose and dressed. It was time to say Mass.

At six o'clock in the school chapel my congregation consisted of seven nuns from a nearby convent. I hurried through the service and at a quarter to seven stood in the vestibule, waiting. Jeannot, like the other boarders, would be at the seven o'clock Mass, which would be said by Father Destouts.

At five minutes past the hour I saw Jeannot come running, among the other stragglers. I stepped out from the shadows beside the Holy Water font, and signalled him to follow me. Behind the chapel there is a cemetery. In it are buried the priests of our Order who died in Ganae. It is small and quiet, shaded by jacaranda trees. In the nearby chapel we heard the shuffling of feet, then silence, as the service began.

'The police were here last night,' I said. 'Do you have any idea why?'

'Was it about the leaflets, Father?'

I remember that I felt both anger and fear. 'Yes,' I said. 'So you're responsible. What sort of nonsense is this?'

'Is it nonsense, Father? You yourself told us it's up to my generation to do something.'

'So what have you done? What will you do? A few schoolboys with no plan and no idea how the world works. All you've done is cause innocent people to be arrested and put in Fort Noël. And do you know what's happened to those people? *Do* you?'

I was shouting. I saw him flinch as though I would strike him. 'I'm sorry,' I said. 'Forgive me, I shouldn't lose my temper. How many of you are mixed up in this thing? And what else have you done?'

'This was just a beginning, Father. It was my idea. We tried to hand the leaflets out to young people—educated young people. If we can make them turn against their parents that will be a beginning. That's why we went to Bellevue and Beaulieu.'

'How many of you are there?'

'For now, maybe ten. But I don't want to give their names.'

'I'm not asking you for their names. Did *you* write the leaflet?'

'Yes.'

There, in the cemetery, the unrelenting sun of the tropics had already mounted its daily attack. We stood in the hot breath of the morning wind while above us the delicate, violet jacaranda blossoms trembled in the moment before their fall. On the worn gravestones I could read the names of our priests, French and Canadian, forgotten now, their labours ended, their bodies rotted to anonymous bones in the unforgiving soil of this lost and lonely land. What was the true meaning of those lives, lived far from France and Quebec? What would be the meaning of my life if I left this island as I found it, still one of the most desolate, despairing places on this earth? But even as those thoughts moved guiltily in my mind, they were driven out by a stronger emotion, one of fear, the fear of a childless Father facing a brilliant black boy who was, to me, a son. Like a father I did not think of principles or causes. I thought of him, of saving him from men in white suits and panama hats.

'Jeannot,' I said, 'listen to me. If those other boys who distributed the leaflets are caught by the police, their parents will intervene. Their parents are the elite and their sons will not be tortured, they will not disappear into prison and never be heard from again. But if you are taken by Doumergue's police, it will be the end of you. And for what? What can you, a schoolboy, do to change things here? Nothing. But if you continue your education and go abroad, then, one day, you may come back with the power to influence events. Tell me. Do you still want to be a priest?'

Behind us, in the church, we could hear the rumble of feet as the congregation went down on its knees.

'Why do you ask me, Father?'

'Because if you do, I'll try to arrange that you be sent to Canada or France to study. There are only certain things we can teach you here. With a mind like yours, that's not enough.'

'And if I do not?'

'Please,' I said. 'Don't misunderstand me. I'm not asking you to become a priest. If you do, you'll be giving up a normal life. And believe me, I will help you in any way I can, no matter what you decide.'

He was silent.

'You don't have to decide now,' I said.

'I have decided. I want to be someone like you. A priest. A teacher. Someone who gives his life for others.'

'Jeannot, you mustn't become a priest because you want to be someone like me. That's not enough. To be a priest you must want, above all, to serve God. That's the only reason. Nothing else will do.'

Again, he was silent. On the path below our feet, tiny lizards whisked over the gravel as though fleeing some unseen enemy. In the church behind us, the Sanctus bell tolled. Instinctively, I bowed my head. And then Jeannot put out his hand and touched my sleeve.

'Christ gave His life for the poor. I want to be like Him.'

'If it pleases God, you will be like Him,' I said. 'But now you must help me. Fifteen innocent people have been arrested. Tell the other boys. This must stop.'

'It will stop,' he said.

TWO

LAST NIGHT, as I was writing, Hyppolite knocked on the door of my room. He brought me a cup of herbal tea. I had not asked for the tea. Perhaps one of the other priests had done so. But Hyppolite is very old. He forgets. No one still expects him to work as our servant. But he has worked ever since the day, forty years ago, when Father Bourque brought him from Meredieu to act as houseman at our residence. Later, I was the one who taught him to drive the school car, something which gave him great joy and raised his status among the other servants. And so he has always thought of me as his special charge. Last night when he brought the tea I was writing down what Jeannot had said to me. 'Christ gave His life for the poor. I want to be like Him.'

I looked up at Hyppolite.

'*Mesiah*,' I said.

He looked at me, puzzled, then smiled, showing his toothless gums. '*Mesiah. Me souviens.*'

Messiah. Of course, he remembers. Which of us, alive in those times, will ever forget that word? But I must not skip ahead, I must write first of those early days when Jeannot was still my pupil. He kept his promise, and I said nothing to Father Bourque. The following year, on my recommendation, our Provincial sent him to Montreal where he became a seminarian and obtained a degree in French literature. At the age of twenty-two, he joined our Order and was ordained as a priest. Because of my duties in Ganae, I was not able to attend the ceremony but I used some money my father had once given me, to buy, as an ordination present, a gold pocket watch with a 'hunter' case covering the dial. Inside the case were engraved his initials, J.P.C. In the letter he wrote thanking me, he said, 'I do not believe that I should ever have or want a beautiful object like this. But I shall keep it with me always to remind me of what you have done for me.'

Shortly after his ordination, our Provincial arranged that he be sent to do postgraduate work at the Sorbonne. He remained in France for two years. At that time I thought I had lost him to the great world. He still wrote every week, telling of his excitement at being in Paris, describing lectures in those crowded classrooms, political demonstrations on the Grands Boulevards, Sunday picnics by the Seine. Yet in each letter he asked for news of the happenings at home. In my replies I spoke angrily, recklessly, about the misery of the poor and the unending cruelties and repressions of Doumergue's regime. At that time I saw no hope of change. In the United States, dictators were still in vogue. Ganae remained a pawn on the international chessboard, a check against Castro, until the time of communism's fall.

This, then, was the future I foretold for Jeannot. He would complete his studies and be sent to teach in Rouen, the headquarters of our Order. Gradually, in the course of time, our relationship would weaken and fade. And then, one morning at breakfast, Father Duchamp said to me, 'I heard something last night which should interest you. I was at dinner at the papal nuncio's house. He said your protégé, Jean-Paul

Cantave, is to become the new parish priest of the Church of the Incarnation.'

'A parish priest? Jeannot?'

'It's true. It seems Uncle D. asked Rome to appoint a black archbishop when Archbishop Le Moyne retired last month. Apparently, the Vatican has agreed. And one of this new archbishop's requests is that your protégé be given a job as parish priest in La Rotonde.'

'But why Jeannot?'

'Because Jeannot wrote to the new archbishop and asked for the job. Strange, isn't it? It doesn't make sense.'

'Now that you mention it,' I said, 'it does.'

But why had Jeannot hidden it from me? Did he think I would try to dissuade him? I felt betrayed but at the same time I experienced a mixture of shame and admiration. The boy I had rescued from the squalor of Toumalie had become the priest I myself had always wanted to be. He had turned his back on the life I led, a life in which I did nothing to dispel the misery I saw around me.

And then, a week after this conversation, Jeannot telephoned me from Paris to tell me he had been awarded his doctorate and was coming home. Hyppolite and I drove out to meet him at the airport. Seven years in northern climates had paled his colour. He looked tired but seemed filled with energy. When he embraced me, holding me tightly in his arms, it was the closest I have ever come to the feeling of joy that a real father must experience when he sees his son after years of absence. And yet I sensed that things had changed between us. From now on, I would no longer be his mentor. I would try to be a helper in his parish of the poor.

As Hyppolite drove us home that first morning Jeannot leaned forward excitedly in his seat, staring out at familiar scenes, crowded, tawdry market stalls, the more marginal vendors crouched on the pavements, *bleus* striding arrogantly across the street, ignoring the oncoming traffic, children running alongside our slow-moving car, holding up bananas in the hope of a sale. As we turned off Avenue de la République, going towards the college residence where the other priests were waiting to give him a celebratory lunch, he said suddenly, 'Can we go first to my new church? I want to see it.'

I told Hyppolite to drive to La Rotonde. 'By the way, *Petit*, I've been meaning to ask you. How on earth did you manage this?'

He laughed. I often called him *Petit*. It was an old joke between us. 'Letters,' he told me. 'I wrote to everybody asking for the job. But the letter that really worked was the one to Uncle D.'

'You wrote to Doumergue?'

'Why not? Friends of mine in Rome tipped me off to the new situation. I wrote saying that I am black and brilliant and I come from the poor. I said my Order would prefer that I teach abroad, but that I want to help him build a new Ganae. Apparently, he had Archbishop Pellerat speak directly to our Provincial. And so, here I am.'

'But Uncle D. will expect you to be his man?'

'That will be his mistake. I want to build a new Ganae with no place for a Doumergue. That's why I came home.'

'*Petit*, you've been away too long. You've no idea what it's like to cross Uncle D. He's Hitler and Stalin rolled into one.'

'And look what's happened to *them*. They're already in the rubbish heap of history.'

'Doumergue is different.'

'Perhaps. But it's not a matter of choice. It's my duty.'

A few weeks after Jeannot joined his new parish I attended Sunday Mass in his church. The congregation overflowed into the aisles. People even sat on the window ledges, high above the nave. I saw at once that they were not only the slum dwellers of La Rotonde. In the centre aisle, jammed together like football supporters at a match, was a large group of street boys, the sort who hang around the airport, trying to carry travellers' bags and offering to find taxis. There were also little islands of our students and I recognised at least five teachers from Le National, the public trade school.

The Church of the Incarnation is an ugly stucco building which looks like a garage, its dun-coloured walls hung with primitive wood carvings of the Stations of the Cross. The choir sings to the sound of an ancient pump organ which is forever out of tune. It is not a church where one would expect to be caught up in the magic and mystery of the Mass. And yet as we knelt, looking up at Jeannot, frail and childlike in a surplice which seemed to have been made for someone twice his size, it was as though he led us into a world from which all other worlds were shut out. As he raised the communion chalice, and in that solemn moment changed bread and wine into the body and blood of Christ, we, who watched, were filled with the certainty that he, by the grace of God, performed a miracle on that altar. I, who have said Mass for forty years, prayed as though I were in church for the first time.

No words I write now can describe my feelings on that morning. When the Mass ended and Jeannot beckoned me to join him in giving communion to the scores who pressed forward to kneel at the altar rails, I looked at their faces and felt that, truly, God had come down among us. I was filled with a happiness I had never known in all my years as a priest. Jeannot had raised me from the grave of my sloth.

Communion had been given. The Mass ended. But the congregation did not rise and leave. They sat in their seats, waiting, as Jeannot climbed the stairs of a rickety pulpit. Looking down on them, he began to speak in a voice that was incantatory, compelling, a voice like no other I have heard. At once, the congregation was silent, rapt.

Brothers and Sisters,
Today I want to raise you up.
The Church is not far away in Rome.

The Church is not archbishops and popes.
The Church is us—you and I—
And we who are the Church have a duty to speak out.
You ask me, speak about what?
I answer. Who are the unholy ones?
They are those who sell your work to foreign countries
And pay you seven per cent of what they get.
Did you know that?

And for the first time in one of our churches I heard the congregation answer in a shout.
'No!'

Brothers and Sisters,
We must begin to speak out.
But I warn you.
If you speak out you will receive blows.
St Paul received blows because he told the truth.
But he endured them.
As you will endure them,
As I will endure them.
Because we must choose the Lord's way.
We must speak out against those who exploit our poor.
We must take the path of love.
The path of love is the path of Jesus.
Help us climb out of this endless poverty.
We do not ask for riches.
We ask to live the lives of the poor
But not lives of starvation and despair,
Not the lives of slaves.
But decent humble lives
Under God.
Jesus asks you
Help each other.
The path of love is the path that leads to justice.
Walk with me on that way.

Jeannot made the sign of the cross and stepped down from the pulpit. And then I saw what I had never seen before. The congregation, behaving as though they were not in a church but in a town meeting, turned to each other, discussing the sermon, some of them clapping others on the back as though urging them on. People rose and agitatedly walked the aisles, while, at the rear, the church doors opened wide as the congregation streamed out into the sunlight, excited, talking, inspired.

When Jeannot came back to the altar, I followed him into the sacristy. I was still filled with that sense of God's presence that had entered the church during Mass. I was certain that this boy who had been my protégé was now a person of exceptional holiness. Yet at the same time I could not reconcile that feeling with the sermon he had preached. It was a sermon of politics. Did he see it as that? Or did he see it, simply, as doing God's will?

'How long have you been preaching like this?' I asked.

'Since my first week. The crowds are getting bigger.'

'But *they* must know you're doing it?'

'Of course they do.'

'*Petit*, you spoke of receiving blows. What if they arrest you?'

'They won't arrest me.'

'How can you know that?'

'Because God is watching over me. Don't be afraid for me. Believe me.'

And I did. In the months that followed I spent all of my evenings in a new community centre which Jeannot had set up in an empty warehouse. I enlisted my students to raise money from their parents so that we could buy furniture, beds and blankets for an orphanage in which the Sisters of Ste Marie were planning to house some of the abandoned children of La Rotonde. I wrote letters to Canada and France soliciting funds for a boys' club and, indeed, such a club soon came into being.

I look back now on those days as a time when I achieved a state of happiness which can only be entered into by a total forgetting of oneself. I forgot my failures, my inadequacies, my guilts. I learned at last to lose that comfortable yet comfortless distance I had felt here, as a white priest in a foreign place, protected from the misery around him by his church and his calling. I worked with Jeannot. Jeannot worked for the people of La Rotonde. Now, at last, I had come to serve the poor.

The crowds grew. The word spread. In the mansions of the elite there was talk of this mad little priest who preached against the rich. Within weeks, when the crowds kneeling outside in the open air rivalled the numbers packed within the church, Jeannot had loudspeakers installed so that everyone could hear the sermon. And the sermon was always the same. Rise up, cast off your chains. You, the poor, will inherit this land.

'I don't understand it,' Noël Destouts said. 'He's preaching revolution. If he were anyone else, he'd be in prison by now.'

Father Duchamp, our resident cynic, saw things differently. 'When Jeannot speaks about capitalists, he's talking about the elite—he's not speaking out against Doumergue. Maybe, he knows just how far he can go.'

I was angered by this remark. I knew it wasn't true. Despite his belief that God would protect him I feared for Jeannot. And then, one Sunday morning, as was now my custom, I attended Jeannot's Mass in order to help him serve communion. The church was packed. I was kneeling at the right side of the altar with my back to the congregation. A few minutes after the Mass began I heard shots which I took for a car backfiring. I heard shouts at the rear of the church. When I turned round I saw six or seven men, armed with rifles and machetes, pushing their way up the crowded aisles, some firing at the ceiling, some firing directly into the congregation. They were not soldiers or *bleus*. They looked like street scavengers, the sort who spend their days picking over rubbish heaps, cadging tourists for handouts, their nights drunk on bottles of homemade *usque*. Two of them had already reached the altar and now, raising their rifles, they fired directly at Jeannot. I saw a bullet strike the gilded door of the tabernacle behind him. A brass candlestick was toppled by a second shot.

Suddenly, it was as though all of us were figures in a painting, frozen in a frame. Jeannot did not flinch. He stood facing the killers, his arms outstretched as if to embrace them. His face showed love, not fear. At this point the marauders in the body of the church ceased firing and, like the rest of us, stood staring up at Jeannot on the altar. Again the two assassins raised their rifles and fired. They were not more than thirty feet from their target, but the bullets went wide. The upraised arm of a statue to the right of Jeannot shattered and fell on the altar steps. The two assassins, unnerved, looked at each other as though unable to believe what was happening. Then, suddenly frightened, they turned and pushed their way back through the crowd. I saw this, I heard screams, as people poured into the aisles, trying to escape. The other assailants, buffeted by the panicky congregation, began to lay about them with rifle butts and machetes as they beat their way back to the church doors. Four teenaged members of Jeannot's boys' club rushed up to the altar and tried to drag him off to the safety of the sacristy. He resisted, standing staring out at the crowd, until the assailants had left the church. Then he turned back to the altar, genuflected, and went down into the body of the church to comfort the injured. I saw an old man dead in a front pew, eyes glazed, blood oozing from his forehead. People were lifting up the wounded and stepping over inert bodies. Women prostrated themselves, weeping, on the corpses of kin.

I heard a dull roar. There was a second roar. I looked up

and saw flames move across the ceiling of the church in a great red rolling wave. I smelled the acrid stink of diesel fuel. I saw Jeannot ahead of me, waving and shouting as he directed the evacuation. Incredibly, in the general panic, his orders were being obeyed. There were screams and shouts, but in the rush to the doors no one was trampled. Under Jeannot's direction the injured and dying were carried out into the sunlight. It was then that I saw police and army trucks lined up opposite the burning church. Soldiers and policemen sat in those trucks, silent and unmoving, as people fled past them, escaping. I looked at Jeannot who knelt near me, holding a dying woman in his arms. I saw him stare back at his church, now ablaze in smoke and flames.

An hour later, when the last of the taxi-buses and ambulances had carried off the wounded, the papal nuncio and a representative of Archbishop Pellerat arrived on the scene. They spoke to Jeannot but not to me and so it was not until nightfall that I found out what happened. Jeannot came to our residence accompanied by a priest from the Archbishop's palace. He told us that the Archbishop and the nuncio had ordered him to move in with us and on no account to return to his parish. This was not, as we first thought, a measure to save his life. Instead, incredibly, it was a form of censure. The facts tell the story. In the days that followed there was no announcement in the press or radio that there had been an attempt on Jeannot's life, that innocent people had been shot and killed, or that the Church of the Incarnation had been burned down. In conversations with the nuncio Doumergue disclaimed all knowledge of the affair, despite the fact that police and soldiers had stood by while the attack was carried out. But, to our surprise and shock, neither the nuncio nor Archbishop Pellerat made any formal protest to the government.

Jeannot was, for those weeks, almost a prisoner in our residence. It was a time when news of what was happening outside came to us only through the street boys who visited us nightly to tell him what was being said in the parish. What was being said was that Jeannot was protected by God. Twice, men had tried to shoot him as he stood at the altar of his church. Each time the bullets had not touched him. He was a prophet, people said. God had sent him to save Ganae. I listened to this talk with mixed emotions. I have always had difficulty believing in the miraculous. But I had long believed that Jeannot was a saintly person, possibly a saint. If that were true, it was conceivable that God had saved him. And, of course, I could not forget the evidence of my own eyes. I had seen the assassins miss, firing at close range.

But what did Jeannot think of such talk? One evening when we were in the sitting room of the residence I asked him. 'What's your idea? Do you think it was a sort of miracle?'

'I don't think about it,' he said. 'There could be another explanation. Perhaps those men were, in some way, afraid to kill a priest and so they aimed badly. Next time they will be even more afraid. If only God's miracle had been extended to those who *were* killed. That's what I think of now.'

Father Bourque was in the room when Jeannot said this. I knew that he had complained to Jeannot about his sermons. I knew that he strongly disapproved of 'those liberation theology priests in South America.' Now, he looked at Jeannot and asked, 'Do you feel guilt?'

'Guilt, Father?'

'You know what I mean. For your sermons.'

'I feel sorrow, not guilt. I think of what Saint Paul said, "Christ lives through me." If I wish Christ to go on living through me I must continue to do His work.'

'Liberation theology is politics, not religion,' Father Bourque said. He rose and left the room.

And then, one morning about two weeks later, when we were breakfasting in the refectory, a servant brought in the morning's mail. I saw Father Bourque pick out a letter with a foreign postmark. He read it, then said, 'I have something here that concerns us all.'

He held up the letter. 'This is from our Father General in Rome. Father General informs me that, after consultations with the Vatican, the Albanesian Order has decided to expel Father Jean-Paul Cantave.'

We sat in awful silence.

At last Noël Destouts said, 'But that's ridiculous, Father! Why?'

Father Bourque continued to read from the letter. 'The reason for expulsion is Father Cantave's refusal to cease preaching sermons that exalt violence and class struggle. These sermons are largely to blame for the tragedy that occurred at the Church of the Incarnation when several parishioners were killed and the church was destroyed.'

Now, at last, he looked directly at Jeannot. 'Furthermore, our General informs me that Archbishop Pellerat has decided that you will no longer be allowed to continue your duties as a parish priest. You are henceforth forbidden to say Mass publicly in any Ganaen diocese. However, as our General points out, you are still a Catholic priest.'

He folded the letter and put it in a pocket of his soutane. I looked at Jeannot. There were tears in his eyes.

'But the Order is my family,' he said. '*More* than a family. You found me, you took me in, you educated me and gave me life as a priest. How can you abandon me now?'

Our feelings, mine at least, were of shame, anger and embarrassment. But Father Bourque, a Frenchman of the old school, showed no emotion. 'I'm sorry,' he said. 'We are all sorry. But, as you know, you have brought this on yourself.'

'Surely that's not true, Father,' I said. 'Burning down Jeannot's church, trying to kill him? How can you say he brought it on himself?'

Father Bourque looked at me coldly. 'Paul, you are not without blame in this matter. I had hoped that you would advise Jeannot against his dangerous course of action. Instead you have encouraged him. However, it's too late for recriminations. This is a sad day for all of us. But, remember, these decisions have been made by our General after consultation with the Vatican and with the Ganaen hierarchy. It's Jeannot's duty to accept them and continue to serve God in other ways.'

'What other ways? What am I going to do?' Jeannot's voice was breaking. He was openly in tears.

'The boys' club and the orphanage were both started by you,' Father Bourque said. 'They have not been destroyed and I'm sure Archbishop Pellerat will permit you to continue your work there.'

'Does that mean my boss is now Archbishop Pellerat—he's Doumergue's creature, he wasn't even appointed by Rome— you know as well as I do—'

'Stop it!' Father Bourque said, sharply. 'I will not have that talk here! You are a priest and you must obey your Archbishop. There is work for you to do. Useful work. I would remind you of the vow of obedience.'

'I'm sorry, Father,' Jeannot said. 'Forgive me.'

He bent his head and sat for a moment in silence. I saw that he was trembling. Then, as if gathering his forces, he said, 'Father, of course you are right. It *is* useful work. But, believe me, it will change nothing here. What good will it do to save a few orphans from the streets, to teach some poor children to read a few sentences, when tomorrow there will be a thousand others just like them? Wouldn't it be better for us to do God's work by helping the poor to force their employers to give them some sort of living wage? Running an orphanage and a boys' club is like bandaging a small cut in a body covered with knife wounds. If we can help the poor to better their lives, *then* we are doing Christian work. That is all I have tried to do. Do the rest of you think it's fair that I be cast out?'

He looked around the table.

'I don't,' I said.

'Nor do I,' said Noël Destouts.

'It no longer matters what *we* think,' Father Bourque said. 'The decision has been made.' He looked coldly at Jeannot. 'What you do now is up to you. You are no longer under my jurisdiction.'

That same afternoon I drove Jeannot with his books and his few belongings to the orphanage that he had recently founded. It was in the Laramie district, some streets away from La Rotonde. He was silent on the journey but when he entered the building and was greeted with joy by the children and the Sisters of Ste Marie who were running the place, he turned to me and said, 'Paul, don't be sad for me. It's not over, it's just beginning. Look at these kids. Unless we stand up against Doumergue and the rich and, yes, the Vatican too, what sort of lives are they going to have ten years from now? Remember—I am still a priest. I don't know what I'd have done if they had taken that away from me. The people of La Rotonde will still think of me as their priest. That's the important thing.'

But Noël Destouts, when I told him this, shook his head and said, 'How can he be a priest if he has nowhere to say Mass and no congregation? It's all over. They don't have to shoot him now. He's finished.'

I don't remember whether I believed Noël. I know that in the weeks that followed I felt that I, too, was finished. I had lost my courage. My days and nights were filled with resentment against Father Bourque and the General of our Order, against the Archbishop, the nuncio and, of course, those cardinals far away in Rome who had condoned a dictator's actions in burning down a church and killing members of its congregation. I felt, as never before, a sense of revulsion at my daily tasks. I stared at my rich mulatto students and saw, in them, their fathers—army officers, industrialists,

Doumerguists—those who had allowed the massacre to take place. I began to spend all of my free time at Jeannot's orphanage and in the boys' club whose membership grew until, on any afternoon, there might be a hundred youths in and around the premises. And, lacking a pulpit, Jeannot preached to them, as he still preached to anyone who would listen.

Then something happened, something obscure and sinister, some convulsion in that hidden inner circle that surrounded Doumergue. One rumour held that it was an attempt by his wife and son to kill his mistress, another that he was revenging himself against a senior officer who had slept with his daughter. But suddenly the nights were filled with the sounds of army trucks on the move, shots fired at random, sirens screaming in the dawn hours. These night moves were taking place not in slums or rural areas but in the elite districts of Port Riche and in Doumergueville, the newly renamed second city of Ganae. For us at the college the first certain sign of unrest was the sudden disappearance of a few of our students. Later we were told that they and their parents had fled the country.

And then, one Sunday morning after an ominous radio silence of several hours, Uncle D. himself was heard on the national radio. He announced in his usual oblique manner that certain snakes had been found to be moving out into the sunlight, waiting to attack any of the poor people of Ganae who walked in their path. These snakes, he said, were yellow-skinned snakes and they had been given added poisonous fangs by certain traitors in the armed forces. But no matter how cunning these snakes might be they could not escape punishment. That punishment had been meted out by the dedicated leader of the Ganaen people, appointed by God to protect the poor. That man, Pierre-Marie Doumergue, had swiftly moved against these snakes and cut off their heads. The nation had been saved and now must give thanks for its deliverance.

Within the next few days, reports came back to us, through priests in Cap Sud, that squads of *bleus* had raided southern villages, burned houses and fired on any peasants who tried to stop the burnings. Jeannot, hearing these reports, spent a two-night vigil alone in prayer in the St Jean-Baptiste Church, a few streets away from his orphanage.

A week after the dictator's broadcast I went up to the boys' club to teach my Sunday class in a literacy programme that Jeannot had started. When I went into the club I saw that fewer boys than usual were using the recreation hall. 'Where is everyone?' I asked Father Cachot.

'Didn't you hear? They say that last night in Papanos the *bleus* massacred nearly a hundred peasants. It was some sort of food riot. They're starving up there. Anyway, the kids here are organising a demo. They're marching on the palace.'

At that moment, we heard shouting in the courtyard. I went out and saw a crowd of people carrying long sticks, which they held like drumsticks, beating them together to create a din. The marchers were not only street boys. There were young priests from various parishes around the city, sisters from the Convent Ste Marie and, improbably, because until now they would have been afraid to take part, a group of the desperately poor residents of La Rotonde. Makeshift banners were being prepared. They held one up.

STOP THE KILLING. JUSTICE FOR THE PEOPLE.

I ran back into the building and into Jeannot's office. Father Cachot was on the phone. 'No, we didn't do it,' he was telling someone. 'It's the kids themselves. I'm trying to find him. Yes, I know.'

'What's going on?' I asked. 'Where's Jeannot?'

'I don't know.'

Suddenly, I had an idea. I ran out again and down the street to the Church of St Jean-Baptiste. When I went into the church I saw him kneeling in a pew in a side aisle, almost hidden from view. His head was bent in prayer. I hurried up to him. 'Jeannot, come quickly. Have you heard about this demo?'

His eyes were closed. He opened them, made the sign of the cross, then, genuflecting to the altar, rose and joined me. 'I didn't start this,' he said. 'I'm praying it will not go badly.'

'But you've got to stop it. Doumergue has outlawed public demonstrations. And they're marching on the palace.'

'I can't. Don't you see? They're defending the poor against violence. It's our duty to help them.'

As we left the church, we heard the long sticks begin to beat a tattoo. The demonstrators had already moved out of the courtyard. Some of the youth club boys, seeing Jeannot, pulled him into their ranks. I went up to him as the procession began to move out on to Avenue de la République. 'Jeannot, speak to them. They could be killed.'

'Paul, you don't have to come. Stay here.'

But, of course, I could not stay. I joined the march. At the start there were perhaps eighty marchers, but as the procession moved into the big Meredieu district, people who came out to watch read the banners and joined the throng. It was seven o'clock in the evening at the end of a burning hot day. As the ranks of the marchers thickened, police and army vehicles were seen moving into the side streets. They did not attempt to block the procession and, within minutes, disappeared as though called back by some central command. Now, the procession was coming to an end of the Avenue de la République which leads into the great square of the presidential palace.

The palace dominates the city. It is a replica of the American White House, but twice as large, a cluster of blindingly white buildings surrounded by formal gardens and high, ornate gilded railings. To reach the palace the marchers must cross the vast empty square that surrounds it, an area forbidden to all but official vehicles. And now, as the sun blooded the evening sky, the marchers were met by the sight of army tanks and weapons carriers blocking the side streets that gave on to the square. As the procession of a hundred and fifty marchers came off the Avenue de la République, army tanks moved in behind them, effectively cutting off their retreat. The marchers, ignoring the tanks, beating their sticks, chanting, 'Stop the killing!', moved boldly across the huge empty square, coming to a halt at the gilded main entrance to the palace. The din and chanting ceased.

I, with Jeannot, was in the front rank of the marchers. As the demonstrators stood there in silence, smartly uniformed soldiers of the Garde Présidentielle appeared in the main courtyard, moving in orderly formation, their rifles at the ready. Leading them, on horseback, was their colonel, who had unsheathed his revolver from its holster. There was no sign of the surly *bleus* who normally lounged around in that courtyard. The main gates of the palace were open. It was a formal confrontation, the President's elite guard, standing inside the courtyard, facing down the mob.

Suddenly, from somewhere behind the marchers, a volley of shots was fired over the heads of the crowd. In fear, I ducked my head. Others all around me cowered down, but Jeannot moved forward.

In a sight none of us will forget, this small insignificant young man, his white cassock dragging the dust behind his sandalled heels, walked slowly towards the opened gates of the palace, the gun barrels of the Garde Présidentielle aimed at him like the rifles of a firing squad. When he entered the courtyard he knelt down, bowed his head and joined his hands in prayer.

There was a moment of total silence. The guards, aiming, looked up at their colonel as if waiting for an order. I saw the Colonel hesitate, then turn and look back at the long french windows on the ground floor of the palace. His horse, fidgeting, made a sudden sidestep as though shying at some invisible object on the ground. The Colonel, steadying his horse, stood up in his stirrups, staring back at the windows as though searching for something there. Suddenly, he barked out a command. The Garde Présidentielle lowered their weapons.

The central set of windows opened and in the red light of the setting sun a stooped figure shuffled out on to the marble steps. He wore a shabby black suit and a battered Homburg hat. As he stepped down, carefully, each marble stair negotiated as though he would fall, he removed his hat and held it by his side. The reddened evening light fell on the bald black skull of an *authentique*, a *noir* as dark as the poorest peasant from Cap Sud or slum dweller of La Rotonde. His face was disfigured by ugly grey blotches or sores. I saw him moisten his lips with his tongue.

The demonstrators stood, transfixed. The only sounds in that vast square were the clacking hoofs of the fidgeting horse and the slow, dragging steps of the dictator as Doumergue walked slowly towards the open gates and the kneeling figure in his path. He stopped directly in front of Jeannot and, looking out over the crowd, made a feeble signalling gesture with his left hand. At once a bemedalled military aide ran out from the palace, carrying a hand microphone, attached to a long coil. Doumergue waited, staring ahead into the red sky like a blind man until the microphone was put into his hand. At that moment he gave his battered hat to the military aide and tapped the microphone with his fingers to see if it was working. The sound of the tap echoed, eerily loud, from public-address speakers high above the palace courtyard.

And now we heard that reedy yet commanding voice, familiar to us as the voice of a relative, speaking in Creole, the common tongue:

'My people. You have come here to talk to me. You have heard bad rumours which are not true. Those rumours are spread by enemies of the poor people of Ganae who know I am their protector. You have come here like children who have been deceived. I am sorry that our enemies have lied to you. Your life is hard. You work hard. This is the Sabbath day, a day of rest for you, and for me. I ask you now. Do not believe these stories. They are not true. Go home. Go in peace.'

Jeannot, still on his knees, looked up at the dictator. 'God has given us the strength to come here. We pray to Him to help us now. If you did not do the killing in Papanos you must punish those who did.'

The dictator stared at him for a moment, then lifted the clublike microphone that he held in his hand and brought it down with a sickening sound on Jeannot's head. Jeannot, stunned, fell forward, sprawling on the ground. At that moment, one of Jeannot's orphans, a fifteen-year-old boy called Daniel Lalonde, broke suddenly from the ranks of the crowd and ran in at the opened gates, his long stick upraised to strike the dictator.

A single shot rang out. The boy staggered, then fell prostrate a few feet away from Doumergue. I saw the Colonel on his horse, the revolver in his hand. Jeannot rose from his knees, went to the boy and bent over him, lifting him into his arms. Blood, spreading from a wound in the boy's neck, spilled on to Jeannot's white cassock in a great crimson stain.

The dictator, still holding the microphone in his hand, said, in a voice which echoed eerily on the loudspeakers, 'Bring him inside.' But Jeannot, carrying the boy, turned away from Doumergue and walked out through the gates. Several of us ran to assist him. When I helped lift the boy from Jeannot's arms I saw that he was dead. I looked back. The presidential guards were closing the gates. The Colonel had holstered his revolver but sat, slumped on his horse as though he had suffered a wound.

Suddenly, Jeannot called to the marchers, 'Go home! Go home! God will avenge us! God will avenge us!'

The marchers were no longer a mob, no longer threatening. They were people, shocked, stunned, frightened by violence. Behind the now-closed gates the dictator shakily remounted the marble steps and reentered his palace. The presidential guards still held ranks, their rifles aimed at the marchers who were retreating, half-running, across the vast empty square.

Jeannot, his cassock soaked with the dead boy's blood, his forehead cut and bruised from the dictator's blow, walked back with me, silent, at the heels of the fleeing crowd. The red sky went black as the sun fell swiftly behind the distant sea.

In darkness, we brought the dead boy home.

THREE

IN GANAE, because of the heat, funerals are sudden. We
buried Daniel at noon on the following day. As Jeannot
was not allowed to say Mass in public, I officiated at the
church. But, at the gravesite Jeannot conducted the burial
service. People covered the cemetery like bees over a hive.
Soldiers, massed in double lines as at a public demonstration,
surrounded the grave. When the cheap plywood coffin was
lowered by ropes into its last resting place, Jeannot, his frail
neck protruding from a white surplice, stepped forward and
sprinkled Holy Water into the pit, then turned to face the
staring military.

'God is *with* us!' he called out. 'God is with *us!*' It was not a
prayer but a cry of defiance and the multitude, hearing it,
repeated it in a disjointed chorus, a rolling thunder in the
noonday heat. Then Jeannot cried, 'But they are killing us in
Papanos, they are killing us in Mele. When, oh Father, are we
going to live in peace?'

Waiting as only he knew how to wait, staring over the
heads of the mourners as though he saw God in the pitiless
noon sky. In that moment of silence, the soldiers stood at bay,
watching this unpredictable figure in their midst. Then, as

though he heard a voice, Jeannot called out, 'And my Father answers me. You will live in peace when you put your faith in a People's Church, a church that will lead a people's revolution, so that our country can breathe free.'

And when he said that, I knew that he had crossed from the City of God to the city of men. This was no longer a religious service for a dead boy. 'God is with *us!*' Jeannot cried again and the people echoed him in a new, excited roar. Instinctively I looked towards the line of soldiers, rifles cocked. Their officers stood silent but the soldiers, one rung up from the poverty of those around them, suddenly joined in the chant.

Jeannot raised his hands as in a blessing, stilling the cries. It was then that an old woman in the forefront of the line of people crowding the soldiers at the edge of the grave went down on her knees and called out, '*Jeannot c'e Mesiah!*' In a growing movement like a wave rolling towards shore, other voices took up the cry. '*Jeannot c'e Mesiah!*' It broke on the last word, swelling into a thunderous sound. *Mesiah.*

Jeannot is the Messiah. I stood beside him on the edge of the grave. He trembled as though in shock, then held out his hand. I gave him the shovel. He threw earth upon the coffin.

Later, as we left the gravesite, we were surrounded by a throng of mourners, among them many of the younger priests and nuns who crowded around Jeannot asking, 'What is the People's Church? Do any of the bishops belong to it? Why have we not heard of it?'

'The People's Church is the church of the poor,' Jeannot said. 'It does not take orders from dictators as do the bishops here. It is a new church and today was its beginning.'

'Can we join? Can we join?'

'You already have,' Jeannot said. 'The bishops' days are numbered.'

As we crowded into the funeral cars that would take us back to Port Riche, I said to him, 'Jeannot, listen to me. First of all, the bishops will try to have you excommunicated. Rome will call this a heretical church. And the minute Doumergue hears what you said about a "people's revolution" he'll lock you up and throw away the key.'

'I've told you. I have no choice. If God has singled me out to do this work, then my fate is in His hands.'

I looked into his face, this boy I had thought of as my son. Saints are people we read about in devotional books. What is a saint? The Church has laid down criteria. Martyrdom is one. Holiness is another. The third is that miracles be connected to that person. Martyrdom? Would he be killed? Miracles? Were the failed assassinations a miracle? Holiness? Yes.

'Anyway,' he said. 'I don't think Uncle D.'s going to arrest me. Why didn't he do it yesterday, at the demonstration?'

'Because you had a dead boy in your arms. Listen to me. Don't go back to the orphanage. Come with me to the college. Noël Destouts has a little place in the hills outside Lavallie. Maybe you can hole up there until we see what happens.'

But he refused. Then, as if to confirm my fears, when we reached the orphanage, a Mercedes was waiting in the street.

'Don't go in,' I said.

He laughed. 'They don't send *bleus* in Mercedes. Come on.'

The front hall of the orphanage was filled with children, noise and confusion. Seeing us enter, one of the nuns came up. 'There is a gentleman waiting for you. He said it's a private matter. I put him in your study.'

When we went into the small, untidy room where Jeannot worked, a man stood with his back to us looking out of the window at the crowded schoolyard. When he turned around I recognised him. He wore a dark civilian suit but I had seen him yesterday on horseback, revolver in hand, dressed in the splendid uniform of the Garde Présidentielle.

'Can we help you?' Jeannot said.

'I'm Colonel Maurras. I've just come from the funeral. Believe me, I didn't go there to spy on you. I went in penance. But I must warn you. Your sermon this morning will be seen as treason.'

He hesitated. 'Father, I know that a man who has shot and killed an unarmed child cannot ask for your forgiveness. I don't deserve forgiveness.'

'Forgiveness comes from God,' Jeannot said. 'And His mercy is infinite.'

The Colonel bowed his head, then said in a low voice. 'You must go into hiding at once.'

'I can't do that. If I'm in hiding I can't do my work.'

'You may not have to hide for long. Doumergue is dying.'

We looked at each other.

'Didn't you see him yesterday? He's in the final stages of AIDS. We were surprised that he showed himself. He lets no one see him, not even his ministers.'

We stared at him. We who had seen so much of AIDS among the poor, why had we not recognised it?

'How long do you think he has?' Jeannot asked.

'A week ago he developed some sort of fever. They have flown in specialists from France. He could go at any time. That's why I advise you to keep out of his reach. He's not dead yet and he's been quite insane these last weeks. He sees traitors everywhere, even in his own family.'

'If he finds out you have come to see us you'll suffer for it,' Jeannot said.

The Colonel turned and again looked out at the crowded schoolyard. Children's cries echoed in the room.

'Nothing matters now. Until yesterday, my life's ambition was to become a general and command a region. But I know that the stain of yesterday will never leave me. I am a soldier, yet the only person I have ever killed is a harmless child.'

He turned back to us. 'Goodbye, Fathers. Be very careful.'

When the Colonel had gone, Jeannot said, 'Perhaps I *should* lie low for a few days?'

'You must. I'll drive you up to Lavallie.'

'No, no, I'll get the boys to take me in their taxi-bus. No one will look for me in a taxi-bus. And while I'm up there I'll make plans to organise some of the younger priests and nuns. We've got to build our own organisation if we're to have a People's Church.'

He must have seen the flicker of misgiving that crossed my face. 'I'm sorry, Paul. I know this is a great leap for you. If you continue to help me you'll be in trouble with the Order. You could be expelled. Perhaps you should stay out of this?'

'No, no,' I said. 'I want to help.'

Four weeks after this conversation, the dictator Jean-Marie Doumergue died and was buried in a state ceremony in the Cathedral of Notre Dame de Secours. The funeral Mass was celebrated by Archbishop Pellerat, head of the Ganaen hierarchy. The papal nuncio was in attendance and conveyed Rome's condolences to the dictator's widow, son and daughter. The Army was represented by, among others, General Antoine Macandal, Chief of the General Staff and acting Head of State. In Ganae on the death of a president, the Army takes over the running of the country, pending elections. General Macandal was a mulatto, as were most of the top army officers who served as members of the military junta. The mulatto elite, newly confident, was prominently in evidence at the ceremonies.

Two days after the interment, Doumergue's widow, son and daughter were secretly flown to France to live out their lives as wealthy exiles on money which the dictator had illegally deposited in Swiss bank accounts. My friend Simon Lamballe, recalled from Cap Nord, told me that the United States had recognised the junta and had agreed not to press for elections until the country was 'stabilised'.

'That's just window dressing,' Simon said. 'Things *are* stable and the Americans know it. Everybody's happy. We're back where we were fifteen years ago, before that *noir* bastard came to power.'

But Simon was wrong. The parliament, a puppet forum during the years of Doumergue's regime, now began to form alliances and demand elections. There were protest marches and demonstrations. And now a new voice was heard on Radio Libre. It was the voice of the People's Church. Jeannot's voice.

One evening I was in the school garage, helping Hyppolite jump-start our old Peugeot, when Father Duchamp ran in, telling me to come and listen. Jeannot was making a speech. When I reached the sitting room, I heard:

One hot meal a week.
Yes, that is what the people eat in Cap Nord and Cap
    Sud.
One hot meal a week. The rest of the week—
I don't have to tell you.
Work all day in the fields and come home to eat
    plantains at night.
But here in Port Riche.
What do the rich eat?
The rich who hold power thanks to the generals.
What do they eat?
Fine French food. Imported meats.
What do they drink?
Fine French wine. Champagne.
They gorge until they vomit.
The poor starve until they retch.
Brothers and Sisters, what is our mission?
It is to enter the temple of privilege
With swords.
To drive these parasites out of our country.

That is what we must do.
That is the work of the People's Church.
You are the Church.
You have the power.
Act.

Father Bourque was not present when we heard that speech. But that same evening he called me into his study.

'Paul, I know this will be difficult for you, but I want you to cut all ties with Jeannot. It's absolutely against the teachings of the Church to incite people to revolt. He's gone off his head. In my opinion he's no longer fit to be considered as a Catholic priest.'

'But the work I'm doing at his orphanage and the literacy classes, none of that is revolutionary, Father. It's useful work.'

'Paul, listen to me. I am going to retire next year. I've already recommended that you succeed me. If you want to change the way things are run, if you want more black students, you'll have a chance to do it when you're in charge here. But if you continue to associate yourself with Jeannot, you'll never be appointed as my successor. In addition, you are risking censure, expulsion from the Order and God knows what else. Please, Paul?'

I said I would have to speak to Jeannot. The next day I went to see him. And, at once, he said, 'Paul, it's all right, it's all right. We need you where you are. You mustn't risk your career at the college. Imagine, if we have a revolution, what a blessing it will be to have you in charge there. Of course, I'll miss your help at the orphanage and at the club. But we'll stay close, you and I. As always. Remember, *Petit* is still your boy.'

'But why do you keep talking about a revolution?' I said. 'The parliament wants elections. Doumergue is dead. For the first time in Ganae's history we have a chance to change things in a democratic way.'

'How? There'll never be democratic elections here, not

while the Army runs things. We need to overthrow the Army and take the means of production away from the elite.'

'And how do you propose to do that?'

'You'll see.'

After this conversation, in obedience to my superiors and to Jeannot's wishes, I distanced myself from his daily operations and so was divorced from the events that followed. Jeannot's broadcasts were heard in every village and hamlet in the country. In Ganae, where eighty per cent of the people cannot read or write, his voice became the voice of a new power, a voice which, by threatening a people's revolution, forced the junta to heed parliament's call for a general election.

René Laberge, one of my former pupils, was now the Member for Pondicher in the General Assembly. He was also the leader of the Social Democratic Party, a newly powerful grouping in the Ganaen parliament. Two months before the general election was scheduled to take place, René came to see me at the college.

'I want to ask a great favour of you, Father. We're hoping to have honest elections for the first time in our history. The trouble is, we have too many parties and none of them is really known to the people. I believe there's one person in Ganae who would win in a landslide. You know who I'm talking about.'

'Yes. But he doesn't believe in elections.'

'That's why I'm here. You're the only person in the world who might make him change his mind. If he doesn't run, the elections will be a shambles and the junta will simply take over again.'

'René, I've promised my superiors to keep my nose out of politics.'

'I know. I've spoken to Father Bourque about this. He says, in this case, it's up to you. Jeannot is down there in La Rotonde talking revolution to slum kids and wide-eyed young priests. With the Army under mulatto control, any attempt at a *noir* uprising will end in failure and hundreds will be killed. There's a way to prevent that, if only Jeannot will run.'

Later that same day I spoke with Father Bourque. 'There's another problem,' I said. 'Jeannot is still a Catholic priest and the Pope has expressly forbidden priests to run for political office. It's important to Jeannot that he remain a priest. A great part of his appeal to the people is that he *is* a priest.'

'Yes, of course,' Father Bourque said. 'And it's true that, if Jeannot runs, the nuncio will report adversely to Rome. But, even so, I think it's worth the risk.'

I had not visited Jeannot's boys' club in some months. When I drove up there the following afternoon, the place looked as though it had been transformed into a campaign headquarters. There were seminarians, young priests and nuns, youth leaders, street boys and others who I did not recognise, at work in each of the six rooms on the ground floor. I saw office desks, computers and, significantly, a room where a crew from Radio Libre was sitting with microphones and sound-recording equipment. In the outer hall there were charts on the walls detailing various demonstrations and parades that were to be held in the next weeks. Father Cachot, until now Jeannot's assistant, had been replaced by 'Pele' Pelardy, a Marxist exile newly returned from New York.

I sensed at once that I was not welcome among these people. But Jeannot, when he heard I had arrived, ran out to greet me. 'Where have you been? Why didn't you come sooner? Let's go up to my room.'

I saw Pelardy look at me with the dislike people of his sort have for priests. 'There's a finance committee meeting,' he told Jeannot. 'They're waiting for you now.'

'Let them wait, then,' Jeannot said. He took my arm and we went upstairs. As we did, I saw a new crush of supplicants waiting in the front hallway. They were people of every sort, the poor of La Rotonde, peasants from the countryside, small politicians, businessmen, students, street vendors. As we moved past them, going up the staircase, faces turned, conversations died to whispers, people waved, hoping to catch Jeannot's eye. Of course I was accustomed to his being the centre of attention. But this was different. I thought of Doumergue. It was as though the awe which Doumergue had inspired had been transferred to Jeannot. He was now the most talked-of man in the country.

Jeannot, typically, ignored all of this. He took me into his tiny, monkish bedroom and closed the door. He went at once to a table and made instant coffee on a heater ring just as he had done in the old days, when we would meet to gossip and talk of his plans.

'What's going on, *Petit*?' I asked him. 'All these people, these meetings?'

'The People's Church is like Rome, it won't be built in a day. I've missed you, Paul. All these people, yes, I'm surrounded. But you're the only one I can really talk to.' He poured hot water into the coffee and handed me a cup.

'I've missed you too,' I said. 'I've missed those days when I could come here and do something useful. But maybe now I can be useful to you in another way. You know René Laberge?'

He laughed. 'Don't say it. I know what you're talking about.'

'He asked me to speak to you.'

'Me, running for president? Ridiculous.'

'Jeannot, listen. There will be international observers at these elections, including the ex-premier of France. That's unheard of, here. And if you run as the candidate of the poor you'll get so many votes that the Army won't be able to rig things against you.'

He started to argue with me. But as we talked, as I kept pressing him, I sensed that he was beginning to change his mind. At last, he said, 'But if I *did* become president I'd alter the system completely. I'd try to take this country out of the hands of foreign capitalists. I'd destroy the power of the elite. I'd get rid of the army officers who run the drug trade. In fact, I'd get rid of the current top brass.'

'In other words,' I said, 'as president you'd make a revolution without having to start by building barricades in the streets.'

'Wait a minute. There's the other problem. The Pope has forbidden priests to run for political office. They'd defrock me, or whatever they call it nowadays.'

'Father Bourque says they might not.'

'But if they did kick me out—look, it's important that the poor know I'm their priest. If I enter politics, all that will end.'

'And if you foment a revolution here, don't you think Rome will see it as taking part in politics?'

He smiled. 'I should know better than to argue with *you*.' He put his arm around my shoulders. 'All right. Tell Laberge I'll think about it.'

A week later we read it in the newspapers. Father Jean-Paul Cantave, 'Jeannot,' the priest of the poor, would stand as the Social Democratic candidate for president.

He went on radio. He campaigned all over the island. On the week of the election, the world media descended on Ganae. International observers were flown in. The Army promised to oversee the polls so that there would be no cheating or disturbances. For once, the Army kept its word. When the results were tallied, Jeannot won seventy-five per cent of the popular vote. The world's press announced that a thirty-year-old Roman Catholic priest had been elected to run the country. Rome was silent, a silence which was interpreted as consent. Seven weeks later, Jeannot was installed as president of Ganae.

On that day, Fathers Bourque, Duchamp, Joliette,

Destouts and I were driven by Hyppolite to the presidential palace. The great square surrounding it was jammed with people. We had to make our way on foot towards the main entrance. The high, ornate railings surrounding the gleaming white buildings were covered by the bodies of slum children who had climbed there for a better view of the courtyard in which the ceremony was to take place. They clung there like human flies, ecstatically screaming, 'Jeann-ot! Jeann-ot!'

In the courtyard amid honour guards, bands, flags and loudspeakers, the Church hierarchy, appointed during the dictator's regime, sat on rows of gilded chairs: behind them were the bemedalled generals of the junta and the leaders of the many parliamentary parties. Facing these dignitaries were row upon row of the elite, men in formal morning clothes, women carrying parasols and wearing bright garden-party dresses. We sat beneath the presidential dais, a small group of priests, nuns and social workers, specially invited by Jeannot. And I—I tell you I was filled with pride as I saw him waiting, small and frail in cheap white cotton trousers and peasant shirt, slack as a puppet on strings until the microphones were readied and the media people signalled that it was time to begin.

And then in that miraculous transformation we had so often witnessed in church, he stepped forward and it was as though some unearthly presence had come down among us. He began to speak, not in French but in Creole, his voice reaching out beyond the capital to the villages, the highlands, the remote places of the island, that voice, electric in its power, humble yet triumphant, the voice of a priest preaching truth. We were caught by that voice and, as the loudspeakers sent it booming beyond the palace gates, the multitude jamming the great square and in the teeming streets adjoining it listened as though they were his congregation. He spoke to them, not to us.

Brothers and Sisters,
At the moment in history,
A moment when
The great revolutions of this century
Are, one by one,
Falling into sad disarray,
At this moment, what has happened here?
Ganae stands on the threshold
Of revolution,
Our own revolution.
Others have failed.
But we will not fail.
We will succeed
Because *our* revolution
Is born not of plans and plots,
It is the voice of our people
Crying out to be free.
We have cried out and God has heard our cry.
That is why we will not fail.
That is why I stand here today.

Abruptly, he stepped back from the microphones, his head bowed, oblivious to the thunder of cheering and the cries of his name.

Gradually the cheers died to silence. There was a small commotion in the official stands. A dignitary stepped forward holding a silken sash bearing the green and gold national colours. He draped the sash over Jeannot's neck and arranged it so that it fell across his chest. Now, Jeannot was the President, the only democratically elected president this black republic had ever known. There was a flurry of applause from the official stands but I saw Archbishop Pellerat and the nuncio exchange glances, as they smiled false smiles. The bemedalled generals clapped condescendingly, nodding to the ambassadors and the distinguished foreign observers who had monitored the polls. The generals were confident. They were the Army. They had made democracy possible, but were still in charge.

The band of the Garde Présidentielle struck up the national anthem. While the music played, Jeannot stood with his hand over his heart in a gesture of patriotic reverence. The anthem ended. Again, there was a flurry of applause. Jeannot stepped forward into the battery of microphones. Those hungry robots, the television cameras, moved in on his face.

Turning to the ex-premier of France who had headed the United Nations observer team, Jeannot thanked him in French, for helping to secure the first free election in the history of Ganae. And then, suddenly switching to Creole, 'Today, as the first act of the People's Government of Ganae, I wish to announce that in my capacity as Commander-in-Chief of the Army I have appointed General Auguste Hemon, Commander at Cap Nord, to be Army Chief of Staff. Again I wish to thank the members of the military junta for their co-operation in helping us form a new government. Now, let our celebrations begin.'

There was a moment of terrible silence in the courtyard. And then, in the square and in the streets outside, a storm of cheering, shots fired in the air, an explosion of fireworks, the chanting of, 'Jeann-ot! Jeann-ot!'

Jeannot turned and walked towards the generals. He moved down the line, shaking each hand, speaking a few words to each officer. I did not hear what was said. No one could, in the din of shouting and chanting outside the palace. General Macandal, a tall, almost white-skinned mulatto, trained at West Point Military Academy in the United States, towered over Jeannot's frail, slight figure. When Jeannot reached him and offered his hand, Macandal began to speak, his features grim, as though he delivered a reproof to an insubordinate sergeant. Jeannot smiled, nodded, and moved on.

A little further down the line he shook hands with General Hemon, his new Chief of Staff, a huge *noir* who, until now, had not been a member of the Army's inner circle. It was my impression that Hemon knew nothing of his promotion until he heard it announced that day.

When Jeannot had completed his tour he joined the UN observers and, as he chatted with the ex-premier of France, a major-domo appeared leading a group of palace flunkies, all of them dressed in ridiculous Ganaen state uniforms in a style that dated back to the eighteenth century, knee breeches, gold-and-white waistcoats, pomaded wigs. The flunkies circulated, holding silver trays filled with glasses of champagne. Champagne in hand, the official party moved to the central courtyard where long tables were laden with every sort of food. I saw the elegant ladies of the elite glance back at General Macandal, then begin an alarmed, excited whispering. Their husbands remained silent, stiff-faced and shocked. The nuncio and the Archbishop engaged in anxious parley as they moved towards the food.

And then, in the second shock of the day, Jeannot, leaving the ex-premier of France, ran ahead of everyone in the official party and, opening his arms in welcome, was surrounded by ragged orphans from his orphanage and some forty or fifty of the poor from the slums of La Rotonde. All wore official badges of invitation to the inner courtyard and had been seated out of sight until the party began. The elite and the generals, shocked and haughty, were nevertheless obliged to mingle with these ragged children and half-starving slum-dwellers who at once began greedily, happily, to devour the rich food.

Outside the palace gates, the huge square was a riot of dancing, cheering and singing. Bottles of *usque* were passed around and large, crude, stencilled portraits of Jeannot were hoisted aloft, his image dancing like a carnival mask above the heads of the people. I stood with Noël Destouts, holding my champagne, my mind going back to a mountain track over which no car had ever driven. A little boy's arms held me tight as the mule picked its way down a steep incline. Behind us on a ramshackle porch, a woman nursed a baby, the woman who had given the boy away as casually as she would give away a puppy from a litter.

And now, suddenly, Jeannot appeared in front of me, wearing the silk sash of the presidency, clasping me to him so joyously that I spilled my flute of champagne on to the ground. He stood, embracing me in front of the generals, the nuncio, the bishops, the ex-premier of France. I heard the elegant ladies, near us, ask, 'Who is the priest, the *blanc*?' But the orphans, the street boys, the poor, did not ask. They knew. They surrounded us, cheering us, giving us their love, as we hugged each other in that unforgettable moment of victory.

FOUR

AT THAT TIME, the Régence was Porte Riche's grandest hotel. It sat on a hill overlooking the city, hidden from view by a phalanx of tropical trees. It was an oasis, closed off, the playground of foreigners, its flamingo-coloured buildings surrounded by formal gardens of exotic flowers and plants. At the rear of the hotel the palm-shaded swimming pool was flanked by an open-air bar at which, every evening, the foreign press, visiting businessmen, and people from the embassies gathered to exchange the rumours of the day. Three weeks after Jeannot became president, I went there for a drink at the invitation of Marc Robin, a Canadian epidemiologist who was visiting Ganae as a member of an international commission on AIDS. We arrived just before sunset. The poolside bar was crowded and we could not find an empty table. But, all at once, a whispering started. Several people got up and ran into the hotel. 'What's happening?' I asked a waiter.

'It's happening now,' the waiter said mysteriously. 'Go and see.'

In the lobby a group of people stood around an old-fashioned black-and-white television set. The sound was not working, although the concierge kept trying to adjust the volume. In eerie silence, interrupted occasionally by electronic squeals, we watched five or six weapons carriers filled with armed soldiers rushing along a country road. The television camera, having trouble keeping up, gave us a glimpse of a large Mercedes racing at high speed. The soldiers in the weapons carriers preceded and followed this automobile as it swung under an archway sign:

AÉROPORT INTERNATIONAL DE PORTE RICHE

At the main entrance to the airport terminal another Mercedes had already arrived. Disembarking from it were two elegantly dressed women, three children and a uniformed nursemaid. As they stood on the pavement, the first Mercedes drove up and a tall, almost white-skinned civilian got out. At once, all of the waiting soldiers and officers saluted. I recognised him: General Macandal. With him was a handsome young man sporting a flamboyant black moustache which gave him the look of a film star of former times. The General hurried across the tarmac, kissed both women, then, taking the arm of the older one, went with her into the terminal building. The nursemaid followed with the children. The handsome man who had accompanied the General began an agitated conversation with the young woman. She was beautiful, light-skinned, chic. I would have taken her for an elegant Parisian. As he talked, she kept shaking her head and when he tried to take her arm, she pulled away from him. At last, angry, he turned and went alone into the terminal. In the background soldiers were carrying several Vuitton trunks through the doors. Other soldiers, their rifles up, guarded this transfer as though the contents of the trunks were valuable. When the television cameras tried to enter the terminal, an officer blocked their way. Frustrated, the crews turned their cameras on the beautiful young woman who had stayed behind.

At that point the concierge managed to restore sound to the television set. She was answering questions.

'No, I am not leaving. This is my country. I won't let that priest push me out.'

'But your husband is going to France, isn't he?'

'Yes he is. You don't know what happened two days ago, no, it was not reported, was it? But those *canailles*, stirred up by the priest, tried to burn down our house. Can you blame my husband if he doesn't want to stay here?'

'So, *you're* not afraid to stay then, Madame?'

'My family built Ganae. My great-grandfather, as you know, was president of this country. I will not let *noir* agitators dictate to me. Now, I must go. Goodbye to you.'

As she said this, her chauffeur held open the rear door of the Mercedes. She got in. The Mercedes drove away.

'Who is she?' I said, to no one in particular.

People looked at me. 'You don't know, Father? That's Caroline Lambert.'

'Who?'

'Colonel Lambert's wife. He was the one with the moustache. You know—he's King Coke.'

And then, at once, the room was filled with speculation. 'So there won't be a coup, after all.'

'Don't be so sure. Macandal can still mount one from abroad.'

'How much did they take out, I wonder?'

'In those trunks or in Swiss bank accounts?'

Everyone laughed.

'Why did France agree to give asylum to Lambert? Macandal, yes—but King Coke? Isn't he under investigation by Jeannot's commission?'

'There's been no trial yet. Nothing has been proved.'

'Lambert will be back. He'll get bored in France.'

'I doubt it,' someone else said. 'I think he was genuinely

afraid of the mobs. Jeannot has been coming on strong about punishing drug lords.'

'And didn't you hear Jeannot's speech on Radio Libre last week? About Caroline, her jet-set friends, her parties, her jewels, her yacht, all of it paid for by King Coke's drug payoffs. It was a brilliant move. Jeannot had to get his mobs out in force. Caroline was the trigger he used.'

I looked at the man who said this. I knew him: Hector Al-Said, a Lebanese, the owner of a furniture factory and one of the few businessmen who had contributed to Jeannot's campaign. 'What mobs, Hector?' I asked. 'What are you talking about?'

'Haven't you heard the rumours? They've been saying the Army will never let him get away with sacking Macandal. So Jeannot sent his people into the streets to show the Army he has real power.'

'People power,' someone said.

'Poor people's power,' Hector said.

Our group began to move away from the television set. Outside, the night lights came on around the pool. I sat with Marc Robin, confused, barely able to keep up a conversation. Jeannot and I had talked several times on the telephone in the weeks since his inauguration. He had not mentioned any of this. Why? Was it because he had entered into a corrupt world of politics and intrigue to which he couldn't possibly admit me? I did not believe that was true. Jeannot had never concealed his actions from me. He was completely honest. He was the sort who speaks out. But now I sat listening to people talk of him in a way I had never heard before. These people, the people from the embassies, the foreign press, the American businessmen, had been expecting his downfall. To-night, to their astonishment, his enemies had fled the country. He seemed to have won. But in the Hotel Régence there was no applause.

· · · ·

Next morning, early, I rang the presidential palace. It was no longer possible to reach Jeannot directly. All calls went through his assistants. My call was routed to Pelardy.

'Is it a personal matter, Father?'

'Yes.'

I waited. After several minutes Pelardy came back. 'Would it be possible for you to meet with President Cantave tomorrow morning? I can schedule it for ten o'clock.'

I told myself that, of course, things had changed. It was no longer possible for us to meet informally, as in the old days. I told Pelardy I would be there.

In the days of Doumergue the interior of the palace was forbidding: empty corridors, vast marbled reception rooms, the silence of a museum in early morning before it opens its doors to the public. But now it resembled a gigantic, noisy courthouse: nuns and priests, social workers, politicians, foreign consuls, street people, a few members of the elite, street merchants, peasant delegations from Mele and Cap Nord, all waited for an audience. Vendors moved through the crowds, wooden trays around their necks, selling sweet local drinks and tiny, bite-sized sandwiches. Where once the dictator's palace flunkies ruled these corridors, wearing white suits, black ties and proper shoes, now, young men in T-shirts emblazoned with Jeannot's picture laughed, beat sticks in local folk rhythms and danced up and down the corridors as they went about their self-appointed task of controlling and ordering the crowds. They knew me from the orphanage. They waved me on.

In a large suite of offices closed off from the rest of the palace I saw a group of people, some at computer terminals, some talking urgently on telephones, some holding discussions in conference rooms. They were the new nucleus surrounding Jeannot, a mixture of professionals and cranks, chartered accountants, environmentalists, civil servants, and a handful of economists and lawyers who had returned from exile in New York and Paris to help build the new Ganae. There was among all of these people a group camaraderie and sense of mission, a carry-over from the recent election campaign in which I had taken no part.

Pelardy appeared, waved to me and led me at once to an inner office where Jeannot was holding audience with whoever was next on his agenda.

Two sergeants of the Garde Présidentielle, big, burly men who had probably been the dictator's bodyguards, sat on cane chairs outside the shut inner door. Pelardy nodded to them and one rose to admit me. Inside, the room was large with an ornate ceremonial desk facing a double set of french windows that looked out on a hedge of pink-and-white hibiscus blossoms. Jeannot sat, not at the desk, but on a small stool in the corner of the room. A ring of empty chairs surrounded him and he was listening to an old woman, possibly a street merchant, who sat facing him. He leaned towards her, his head bent, his right hand covering his eyes as though he were hearing her confession. The old woman talked agitatedly, her voice high and angry, the Creole words jumbled so that I could not hear what she was saying. Was she denouncing someone? Jeannot leaned close and whispered to her, stopping her tirade. Rising, he put his hand on her head in a gesture of benediction. Stiffly, she got to her feet. Obedient, she took her leave of him. As she went towards the door, she saw me, stopped, and whispered, 'C'e Mesiah, c'e Mesiah. Deu même, t'entends?'

Jeannot came towards me, smiling. He looked at the old woman who was now going out of the door. 'What did she tell you?'

'That you're God Himself. What's the matter, *Petit*? Isn't it enough to be President?'

He laughed and led me across the room, seating me on the chair facing his little stool. 'I suppose you've come about the nuncio?'

'The nuncio?'

'You mean you haven't been told?'

'No. What?'

'He left for Rome on Saturday. I thought he'd gone on holiday, but now I hear he's been recalled for good. Which means the Vatican isn't going to recognise my government.'

'But that's incredible.'

'Not at all. Rome has been told that if I remain in power I'll start a heretical, breakaway church. Any day now, I expect the Vatican will announce that I'm no longer a Catholic priest. And what will I do then? I can fight the Army, I can fight the elite, but I can't fight Rome. The Pope may be my enemy but still—he's the head of the Church.'

He rose and walked to the window. Outside in the morning sun a tiny green hummingbird, its wings beating at invisible speed, poised immobile over an hibiscus flower. As Jeannot moved to the window, the hummingbird switched its tiny head, saw him, and flew off into a blaze of sun.

He stood, his back to me, looking out of the window. 'This is the worst possible time for me to have trouble with Rome,' he said. 'We're just getting started here. The first thing is to try to improve people's working conditions. And to do that we must make the employers afraid of us. Otherwise they won't change a thing.'

'Is that why you sent mobs into the streets last week?'

He turned away from the window and asked angrily, '*What* mobs in the streets? Is that what they're saying? I didn't put mobs in the streets. The people have taken to the streets themselves. They see that those who helped the dictator are still in power. They're asking that these people be punished. I was elected by the poor. I must heed their demands.'

'What does that mean?'

'It means arrests. And trials.'

'Jeannot, listen to me. Arrests and trials will not put food in people's mouths. What will you do if foreign investors pull out of Ganae? You need trade, you need tourism, you need new investment, new jobs.'

'I see,' he said bitterly. 'Now, we will have the American aid lecture. Calm down. Let the poor be exploited. Aid will follow. I don't want that sort of aid.'

'Neither do I. But you won't change conditions here through denunciations and revenge. It's going to take a lot more than that.'

'Paul,' he said. 'I thought you were my spiritual advisor, not my campaign manager. What do you know about politics?'

'Not a great deal. But perhaps more than some of those dreamers I see sitting in your outer office. You've been given power, Jeannot. For God's sake, use it wisely.'

'For God's sake?' His eyes, those extraordinary eyes, widened in anger. 'Was I elected to do things for God's sake, or for the sake of the poor of Ganae? Aren't they the same thing?'

'That's simplistic.'

'Maybe.' He was silent for a moment, then bowed his head, covering his eyes with his hand, rocking to and fro on his stool. I recognised the signs. I went to the door and opened it. The presidential guards rose from their chairs. Behind them I saw Pelardy talking on the telephone. I told him what had happened. At once, a flurry of people began moving in and out of Jeannot's study. Sister Maria, a nun who had trained as a medical doctor, gave him some tablets and a glass of water. She ordered the shutters drawn. I waited outside with the others. Telephones rang. Pelardy was postponing Jeannot's appointments. After a few minutes, Sister Maria came out. 'He's asking for you.'

When I went back into the room he was lying on a couch, well away from the light. 'Come, sit by me,' he said. 'I'm sorry about this.'

'Did I bring it on?'

'The migraine? No. It's been waiting for me all morning. Paul, please forgive me for speaking to you like that. But there *is* a plot to bring me down. Can you imagine the range of our enemies? Archbishop Pellerat, King Coke, the elite, Macandal. What a team! And now they're going to bring the Vatican into it. If the Vatican strips me of my role as a priest it could do me more damage than any other factor in this mess. Is there any way you can find out what's happening in Rome?'

'I could try.'

'Will you?'

'Of course.'

As though he had been listening outside the door, Pelardy entered the room to say that Ganae's ambassador in Washington was on the line. I took my leave.

At the residence that evening Father Bourque confirmed that the nuncio had been recalled to Rome. 'I only heard of it yesterday,' he said. 'Something's going on. I was told that the Archbishop also went to Rome last weekend.'

'Do you think this means the Vatican will move against Jeannot?'

'The Archbishop will certainly advise them to disown him.'

I went up to my room that night, planning to ring Jeannot in the morning and tell him about the Archbishop's departure. I had undressed and was getting into bed when Hyppolite knocked on my door. 'There is a Monsieur on the phone who say he is your brother.'

I thought it would be Jeannot calling incognito. But when I went downstairs, the voice on the phone was Henri's, far away in Ville de la Baie, Quebec.

'Paul, *Maman* has had a massive coronary attack. The doctors say there's no hope she'll survive it. She keeps asking for you. She told me to ask you to come at once. Is that possible?'

'Yes. Where is she? What hospital?'

'She's at home. She wanted to come home and the specialist says at this stage it won't make any difference. She's conscious, though, quite clear in her mind. And, as I say, she keeps asking for you.'

I told him I would leave in the morning. I went back to my room and took from under my bed the flat tin trunk that contained my winter clothing. The black serge suit and heavy winter overcoat looked as though they had once belonged to some larger, more confident man. As I laid them out I remembered that the flight was at seven A.M. I must reach Jeannot tonight to tell him about the Archbishop and about my leaving.

And so I went back downstairs and rang the palace. After a delay, Sister Maria's voice said, 'He's asleep, Father. Is it urgent?'

'I'm afraid it is.'

'I'll wake him.'

A few minutes later the silence of the telephone line was broken by a whispered voice. 'What is it, Paul?'

'I have to go to Quebec first thing tomorrow morning. My mother is dying.'

'Oh, Paul, I'm sorry.'

'I just wanted to let you know that Archbishop Pellerat left last weekend for Rome. I don't know why.'

'Who told you this?'

'Father Bourque. He also said that Pellerat will advise the Vatican to disown you.'

He was silent. Then he said, 'Is there any hope for your mother?'

'I'm afraid not. But she's asking for me. I feel I must go.'

'Of course. Paul, hurry back. I'll need you.'

And was gone.

Next morning, wearing the heavy winter clothing that no longer fitted me, I was driven to the airport by Hyppolite. There, I bought a return ticket to Miami with ongoing connections to Montreal. When I handed in my passport at the desk of the Police de Sécurité the policeman checked it against a list and then, to my surprise, asked me to wait. I watched him go to an inner office and speak with a sergeant. The Sergeant came out to the front desk.

'May I see your tickets?'

I gave him my tickets.

'Are these all of the tickets? No other destination?'

'No.'

He went back into the office and picked up a phone. I watched, but could not hear what was said. He returned to the counter, stamped my passport with an exit visa and handed passport and tickets back. *'Bon voyage, Mon Père.'*

As I waved goodbye to Hyppolite at the departure gate I told myself that Doumergue was dead and the junta was no longer in power. This was Jeannot's Ganae. Why, then, was my name on a list? Why was I asked about my final destination? Did he not believe I was going to visit my mother? Even under Jeannot, would nothing ever change here?

My plane, turning in an arc, passed over the abandoned buildings of the Bicentennial Exposition Grounds, that symbol of Ganae's efforts to imitate other, more fortunate lands. But the people of Ganae know no other lands. They live in a world apart. Even to me as I flew away from it, its endless struggles, its cruelties and despairs seemed a tale so frightening that, if I told it, no one would believe that such a place existed. My plane, as though confirming this, flew over the white froth of surf that rings the fouled beachfront, leaving the island behind us, wiped out like a chalk mark on the great green blackboard of sea.

That evening I was met in Montreal by a young seminarian from the Collège St Luc where I had studied when I was his age. I was driven through well-lighted, snow-swept streets, past tall gleaming buildings and an affluence of every sort, to the grounds, chapel and classrooms of the seminary where my fellow-Order priests were waiting to give me supper. Next morning, shivering in sub-zero temperatures, I flew to the town of Chicoutimi, two hundred miles north of Montreal. On the plane, listening to the familiar French accents of my native Quebec, my life's choice came back to haunt me. What if I had stayed in Ville de la Baie and become a doctor like my father and my brother? I thought of that life I would never know, a life lived with a woman, a life with children of my own. And then, as though presenting me with my alternative self, the first person waiting for me at the arrival gate was Henri. We hesitated. We were never demonstrative in our family, but was a handshake enough after sixteen years? Awkwardly, we embraced.

'How is *Maman*?'

'She's still conscious, still waiting for you. Frankly, we think that's what's keeping her alive.' Suddenly he broke off and pointed to my shoes. 'Don't you have snow boots or rubbers? Your feet will be soaking.'

And with that remark he established our long-held positions. He, the older brother, responsible, provider for his mother, his wife and his children. I, the impractical younger brother who have lived my life under the protective shelter of a religious order. I knew at once that he would drive us to the nearest shopping mall where he would select for me heavy socks and boots and would expect to pay for them.

'How much is that?' he asked, handing his credit card to the salesman.

'Wait. I'll get it.'

'What's happened to the vow of poverty?'

'Times have changed.'

'You mean the Order pays you now?'

He intended no insult. To Henri, religion is part of the social contract. I would guess he has not thought of God in many years. I smiled and took a hundred-dollar US bill from my wallet. At once, he warned me. 'Be sure they give you the proper rate of exchange.'

Twenty minutes later, driving on the road to Ville de la Baie, we reached the great snow-covered fjords that enclose the Saguenay River. It is a road I remember well for at the end of it is the lumber yard founded by my grandfather. As we passed by I looked for the old sign: BOIS DE CHARPENTE—MICHEL, but instead saw a new and ugly billboard: QUINCAILLERIE DE LA BAIE.

'Hardware?' I said to Henri. 'What's happened to the lumber business?'

'It's secondary now. Times have changed, remember?'

But had they really? We drove into the town and it was as though I had never left. I saw the familiar white-painted wooden houses, the wide front porches, the high, slanting roofs. We passed through the commercial streets of the town with their old-fashioned shop fronts, higgledy-piggledy corner grocery stores and the Quebec Liquor Commission outlet, its floors piled high with cartons of beer. We reached a quiet square. Standing alone in a white rectangle of untrodden snow, was the grey stone church with its tall silver spire where I, an eight-year-old altar boy, served my first Mass. Had anything changed here? I remembered *Maman* telling me about the Great Depression when hungry families queued for free soup and men went door-to-door looking for a day's work. But what did they know of despair? No one starved, no child played in filthy water, no one's twelve-year-old daughter offered herself for sale. What if I had been an altar boy in La Rotonde?

We drove into Rue du Fort. Half-way down the street was the house where I was born. Several cars were parked outside and when we walked up the narrow, snow-cleared path to the front door I saw a jumble of overshoes in the hall, a sign that there were many people inside. In the front sitting room were my sister Justine, her husband Robert, Aunt Marie, Aunt Isabelle and many people whom I did not know. I was embraced and introduced, offered coffee, told that I could not see *Maman* just yet as the doctor was with her. I sat, half-hearing what was said to me, my eyes fixed on a familiar oleograph of Christ crowned with thorns. I remembered, as a child, sitting in different parts of this room, trying to avoid that portrait's stare. But, no matter where I moved, His eye was on me.

A uniformed nurse appeared and said that I could go up. When I went out to the hallway a young man was coming downstairs. He smiled at me and, putting his hand on my shoulder, said, 'I'm Dr Pouliot. It's wonderful that you managed to get here in time. I'm afraid it won't be long now.' He pressed my arm and, as he moved away towards the overloaded coat rack in the hall, the nurse beckoned me to follow her upstairs.

My mother's bedroom was as I remembered it from childhood. There were two painted statues on the mantelpiece, one of Jesus, one of Mary. A red votive lamp burned between these effigies and the room itself had a faint, sickly smell, reminiscent of stale flowers. In the high, old-fashioned bed in which I was born, my mother lay, surrounded by pillows and cushions. She was tiny in age, her skin translucent, as though lit by some flame flickering within her body. When I kissed her I saw that her white hair now barely covered her pink, domed skull. I sat down beside her, holding her hand.

'*Maman*, it's me. Paul.'

When I spoke, she looked up, as though seeing me for the first time. Easing her hand free of mine, she lay back on the pillows, her breathing suddenly harsh. I looked at the nurse who hovered behind us but the nurse smiled reassuringly. 'It's all right, Father. I'll leave you now.'

My mother watched the door close, then pulled herself up into a sitting position.

'Paul, I couldn't . . .' She stopped, in mid-sentence. 'Paul, I want to ask you . . .'

'What is is, *Maman*?'

'It's the end for me.'

'No, no,' I said, foolishly.

'Father Demarais has given me the last rites. So I know it's over. Paul, I'm afraid.' She began to weep.

'Don't be afraid,' I told her. 'No one wants to die, but no one is more ready for death than you are. Soon, you will be in heaven.'

When I said that, she lifted her head and stared at me. Her face was the face of a stranger, frightened, despairing. 'No, Paul, no!'

Was there some sin, real or imagined, which made her think this? 'Why, *Maman*?'

'Do you remember when you were a little boy and did something bad? I would say to you, "Remember, Paul, the Man Upstairs is watching you." Do you remember that?'

'Of course I do.'

'I was wrong to tell you that,' my mother said. 'There is no one watching over us. Last week, when I knew I was dying, I saw the truth. Paul, I have prayed all my life. I believed in God, in the Church, I believed I had a soul that was immortal. But I have no soul. When we die, there is nothing. That's why I sent for you. I must speak to you—you of all my children. Paul, listen. You must give up the priesthood. When I think how I guided you towards it, when I think of the times I told you how happy it would make me if you became a priest. If it weren't for me you might be a doctor doing useful work like your father and Henri. You'd be married, you'd have children. You would not have wasted your life telling people something which isn't true. Please, Paul. You're forty-seven years old. It's not too late. Promise me. Leave the priesthood now.'

'*Maman*, you're wrong. You didn't make me a priest. I was the one who decided it. And you will go to heaven. You *will*.'

'No.' She lay back on the pillows, her eyes not on me but

on the red votive lamp flickering between the painted plaster statues on the mantelpiece. 'There is no other life,' my mother said.

Again, I reached for her hand and held it, the skin loose as a glove over her small, aged bones. Words of pious reassurance stumbled through my brain, mechanical as a doctor's promise that what is about to happen will not cause pain. There are things one says to those who fear death, whose faith is weak, whose courage has forsaken them. But they would not help my mother. Her words mocked all pretence. I raised her hand and kissed it, that hand which had fed and washed me, which had lifted me from my crib. She tried to speak but, instead, gasped and coughed, her breathing harsh and shallow. Speechless, she stared at me in desperate pleading. I rose, ran to the door and called the nurse. In a moment the room was filled with people. As they moved her in the bed, her nightgown twisted about her shoulders, revealing her withered breasts. I averted my eyes and, facing the mantelpiece, saw, as though in mockery of her agony, the painted statue of Jesus, its index finger pointing towards the bleeding heart painted on its breast. Below the statue the flame of the little red votive lamp flickered behind its heart-red glass. Soon, this room would be empty. Someone would blow the flame out.

Later that afternoon, we family members knelt around her bed to recite the rosary. I led the prayers. Facing me, Justine prayed, her head bowed. She was forty years old, the mother of a boy and two girls. Henri, dutifully mouthing Hail Marys at the foot of the bed, was also a parent. Were her children and grandchildren the only true continuation of my mother's life? I looked at *Maman's* dying face, her eyes shut tight, her breathing harsh as she fought to fend off that absence which had already entered the sickroom. *There is no other life.* My voice continued to recite the familiar prayers. The rosary ended, we rose and left the room. When next I saw my mother it was at six o'clock that evening in answer to an urgent summons from the nurse. We crowded into the sickroom. Faces turned to me, waiting for me to raise my hand in blessing and pray for the repose of my mother's soul. I made the sign of the cross but found I could not speak.

On the island of Ganae the night is never silent. In the slums that adjoin our residence, there are no cars or trucks and so the noises of night are medieval. Voices quarrel, shout, sing drunken songs. Dogs bark. Roosters, wakened untimely, crow in darkness. Footsteps sound loud in the narrow, filthy streets below my bedroom window.

But that night in Ville de la Baie, as I lay in the attic bedroom of Henri's house, the only sound to be heard was a soft plop as a slab of melting snow slipped off the high, sloping roof above me to fall into deep drifts in the garden below. In a funeral parlour three streets away, my mother's body waited burial, her voice stilled, that voice which, in sixty-seven years of daily prayer, praised and honoured a God who, in her last hours, deprived her of that ultimate consolation of religion, belief in a life after death. Until now, nothing my mother had ever said or done would have made me suspect she could harbour doubt. Nor were her dying words the panic of someone facing the mystery of death. She had been as certain in her unbelief as, all her life, she had been certain in belief. In the darkness and silence of that night before her funeral, a sad and terrible question crept into my mind. Why did God fail her at the end?

Next morning I said Mass for the repose of her soul. Afterwards, funeral cars drove us out of the town along the ice-sealed banks of the Saguenay River to the Cimetière St Martin, its gravestones like scarecrows in a white waste of snow. There, hard permafrost earth had been spaded up from my father's grave to make room for my mother's coffin. As we stood, a small deputation of the living in that white field of death, I thought of another funeral, four years ago, the funeral of fifteen-year-old Daniel Lalonde, shot down by a colonel of the Garde Présidentielle. Again I heard Jeannot's defiant voice as he stood over the grave. 'God is with us!' Was it a warning to those who would oppress the poor? Or was it a cry of despair, calling on a God who may not be there?

Hard clods of earth fell like stones on my mother's coffin. Father Demarais sprinkled Holy Water on her grave and spoke the final sentence. 'Remember, man, that thou art dust and unto dust thou shalt return.' Were those words her true obituary?

'But you're not leaving so soon?' Justine asked me. 'Surely you can stay one more night?'

We were in her house. Most of those who were at the funeral had been invited back for coffee. A boy and two girls, my nephew and nieces, were handing around plates of sandwiches and plum cake. They smiled at me familiarly, those young strangers, as did many others who greeted me in the expectation that I would remember them. But I did not. Sometimes a name came back and I looked at a face in alarmed curiosity, trying to discern the lineaments of a boy or girl who was once my friend. I smiled, I made the small change of conversation, an actor in a role I could no longer play. Now that my mother was dead, I would not come here again.

'I'm sorry,' I told Justine. 'But it's mid-term at the college. I must get back.'

I signalled to Henri who was waiting to drive me to the airport. As we put on our overshoes in the hall, one of my nieces ran out to tell me that there was a telephone call. 'A Father Monceau. He's calling from Jamaica.'

Father Monceau was our Provincial for the Caribbean area.

'I've been tracking you down,' he told me. 'How is your mother?'

I told him I had just come from her funeral.

'I am very sorry,' he said. 'May she rest in peace. I'm afraid I've called you for another reason. I wanted to reach you before you returned to Ganae. I've been asked to send you to Rome at once. I think it will be easier for you to fly directly from Montreal.'

'Rome, Father?'

'Cardinal Innocenti, who is Prefect of the Congregation for the Clergy, is conducting an investigation into the case of Father Cantave. Archbishop Pellerat is already in Rome. Will it be possible for you to get to Montreal tonight?'

'As a matter of fact, I'm on my way there now.'

'Good. Then you could be in Rome by tomorrow evening. If so, you'd be ready to meet with the Cardinal on Saturday.'

'Yes, Father.'

'One more thing. This hearing is informal and confidential. At this time it's better that Father Cantave doesn't know about it. Do you understand?'

'Yes, Father.'

'Good. Well, safe journey. Oh—I will remember your mother in my prayers.'

FIVE

'THE CARDINAL has little English,' Monsignor Giobbi informed me. 'He has fluent French, so the proceedings will be conducted in that language. Especially as Archbishop Pellerat will be present. My own French is rather rusty. I may have to rely on your help.'

Monsignor Giobbi was the head of our house in Rome and a professor at Gregorian University where, among other subjects, he sometimes lectured on South American liberation theology. Monsignor Giobbi, a Sicilian, did not reveal his thoughts. I did not know if he was accompanying me as the head of our house or as a witness for or against Jeannot.

It was nine A.M. Across Rome on the stroke of the hour church bells rang out, calling the faithful to worship. The doors of the Vatican ante-room opened and Father Sykes, an English priest who was the Cardinal's secretary, beckoned us to follow him. He led us down a long corridor lined with portraits of cardinals from another age and opened the doors of a large, high-ceilinged drawing room. It was winter in Rome. Under an ornate mantelpiece, a fire burned in a huge grate. Around the fire were grouped armchairs and a sofa, covered in blue brocade. Seated there were four clerics, all of whom looked up as we entered. Cardinal Innocenti rose, peering at me over gold-rimmed half-spectacles. He was a small, stooped man in his seventies, his silver hair almost shoulder-length beneath his crimson skullcap, giving him the look of one of those medieval cardinals whose portraits we had seen in the corridor. The other clerics rose, following his lead. One was black, tall, a bald eagle who stared at me with no word of greeting. And yet he was my Archbishop, Étienne Pellerat, head of the Ganaen hierarchy. Monsignor Rinaldi, the papal nuncio in Ganae, nodded to me but did not speak. The Cardinal and the fourth cleric, an unknown monsignor, greeted me in Italian.

I was nervous. I had never been in the Vatican before, other than as a tourist. A white-gloved servant appeared, carrying a tray with cups of espresso. The Cardinal, switching to French, invited me to sit with him on the sofa, thanking me for coming and saying I must be tired from my long journey. He then turned and nodded to Father Sykes who opened a leather-bound dossier and, speaking directly to me and to Monsignor Giobbi, said, 'The Cardinal has called an inquiry today into the case of Father Jean-Paul Cantave. As most of you know, Monsignor Rinaldi has been recalled here by the Vatican Secretariat of State. For the moment, the post of nuncio in Ganae is vacant and the Holy Father has decided that it will not be filled until we have clarified matters there. His Holiness has based his decision on a report furnished by Monsignor Rinaldi. Archbishop Pellerat has recently read this report. Therefore, I think we will begin with the Archbishop's comments on the situation.'

He turned to Pellerat. 'If that is convenient for Your Grace?'

Pellerat rose and stood with his back to the fire. He bowed slightly to the Cardinal. 'Eminence, in Ganae we are facing a crisis which is not only political but religious. To discuss, first, the religious aspect. Since Cantave's election to the presidency, he has gathered around him a number of younger priests and nuns who think of themselves, not so much as members of the Catholic Church, but members of Cantave's church, the "People's Church" as he calls it. These young people, inspired by his rhetoric, have embraced the doctrines of "liberation theology" which, as you know, often advocates revolutionary action to overthrow established governments. These young clerics have no faith in the parliamentary process or, indeed, in democracy. They are, in fact, turning the poor against their pastors if those pastors refuse to embrace Cantave's doctrines. So we have now in Ganae a schismatic church, which is advocating a break with Rome.'

The Cardinal looked at Monsignor Rinaldi, the nuncio, as if for guidance. 'But from *your* report, Monsignor, I was under the impression that it is not a break with Rome but a break with the local hierarchy which Father Cantave is trying to foment?'

'That is true, Eminence,' the nuncio said. 'The hierarchy, as you know, was appointed not by the Vatican but by the dictator Doumergue and, unfortunately, in the backlash against Doumergue's regime the Ganaen bishops are perceived by the poor, erroneously of course, as supporters of the former regime.'

I looked at Archbishop Pellerat and saw that he was stiff with ill-suppressed anger. 'I beg to differ with Monsignor Rinaldi. I think I know our people better than he does. The people respect our views, and indeed, they revere the episcopate. Yes, our appointments were proposed by President Doumergue. But I would remind you that all of those appointments were ratified by the Vatican.'

'Of course, of course,' the Cardinal said. 'The appointments were, as you say, agreed to by His late Holiness. Now —you mentioned the political aspect?'

'The political situation is this,' the Archbishop said. 'Cantave has been president for four months. In that time he has consistently fought with parliament, vetoing not only its legislative proposals but also its recommendations for the appointment of ministers, ambassadors, etcetera. He has surrounded himself with left-wing exiles who are openly hostile to the business interests of the country. He incites the people to violence and threatens to put members of the country's elite on trial for what he calls "crimes against the poor." Ganae is on the brink of chaos.'

'What are the possibilities of his being overthrown?' the Cardinal asked.

The Archbishop shrugged. 'Coups are a fact of life in Ganae. At the moment Cantave is protected by General Hemon, the Army Chief of Staff who is his appointee. If some officers decided to challenge Hemon, then . . .' Again, he shrugged.

'There is another important factor,' the nuncio said. 'He is a hero to the great majority of the poor. They call him their "Little Priest." In my view, if you were to force him to choose between being their priest or their president, you would put him in a difficult position.'

The fourth cleric, the one I took for a Vatican diplomat, now spoke up. 'Eminence, our information is that, if forced to choose, he will, of course, choose the presidency.'

'I'm sorry,' the Cardinal said. 'Monsignor Pecci, excuse me. I haven't introduced you. Gentlemen, this is Monsignor Pecci of the Second Section of the Secretariat of State.'

I looked at this stranger. The Vatican Secretariat of State is, in effect, the Vatican's diplomatic service. Its influence is immense. It must have been Pecci or his superiors who had decided to withhold recognition.

The Cardinal, sitting beside me on the sofa, peered at me through his gold-rimmed spectacles. 'Perhaps, at this point, we should hear Father Michel's views. I am told that Father Michel has a great influence on Father Cantave, perhaps greater than anyone else. Is that so, Father?'

I was sick with tension. When I began to speak my voice was anxious and angry in a way that made me seem unstable. I began by saying that I did not feel that I had any special influence on Jeannot. 'I am his friend,' I said. 'I believe him to be one of the most honest young men I have known. He is deeply religious and when he was expelled from our Order it was one of the great sorrows of his life. Monsignor Rinaldi is right when he says that forcing him to choose between the priesthood and the presidency would place him in a great dilemma. Father Cantave did not seek to become president of Ganae. He was an unwilling candidate and only agreed to run when persuaded by others that if he did not the elections would be a sham. Both before and since his election he has consistently fought for the rights of the poor. He has many enemies and has survived an attempt on his life. His church was burned down and his parishioners killed. Because of these things the people trust him implicitly. The overwhelming vote he received is proof that the poor of Ganae have lost all faith in their former leaders and, unfortunately, this includes the clergy who were silent during the years of the dictator's rule. Father Cantave is the voice of the poor and their voice should surely be heard. I would suggest that now is the time for the hierarchy and the nuncio to forget their previous strictures against him and try to come to terms with the new situation that has arisen. The People's Church is *not* a schismatic church but part of the Catholic Church. It should not be ignored or disparaged. We should try to unite the Church and the people of Ganae behind this new democratic government. Has there ever been a clearer case of doing what the Pope himself has asked us to do: opting for the poor of this world?'

When I sat down, the Cardinal asked Monsignor Giobbi, 'Monsignor, is there anything that you wish to add to what has been said?'

'I tend to agree with Father Michel,' Giobbi said. 'I believe we should try to reach some sort of peace with Father Cantave.'

The Cardinal turned to the Archbishop. 'Do you have any further comment at this time?'

'Yes. I totally disagree with Father Michel. Cantave *is* trying to found a schismatic church and unless he is disowned we will have a state of religious chaos in Ganae. In my view he should be excommunicated.'

'Thank you, Your Grace,' the Cardinal said. He rose from the sofa and walked towards the fire where he stood warming his hands. I looked at his stooped back, long silver hair and crimson skullcap, at the broad crimson sash wound around the middle of his black soutane. What was he thinking? He leaned further into the great fireplace, rubbing his hands together, then stretching his long fingers towards the flames. Monsignor Pecci, the Vatican diplomat, looked over at Father Sykes, raising his eyebrows in question. Father Sykes smiled non-committally, closed his leather folder and sat, composed and waiting.

The Cardinal nodded his head towards the flames, as though listening to some argument which only he could hear. At last, still chafing his hands, he turned to face us. 'First let me say that, at the moment, I do not see a reason for excommunicating Father Cantave.'

'But surely, Eminence—' Archbishop Pellerat was so angry he could barely control his voice. 'Isn't it true that he deliberately disobeyed the Holy Father's order that no priest be allowed to take up political office?'

The Cardinal smiled. 'The law of the Church in Canon 287 states that clerics are not to assume an active part in political parties unless the need to protect the rights of the Church or to promote the common good requires it.' Again, he smiled. 'I quote from memory, of course. But let me emphasise that any such decision can only be taken by the competent ecclesiastical authority. At this moment, I am that authority. I have heard your views and I thank all of you for giving them to me and for the trouble you have taken in preparing them. I will consult with Cardinal Ludovici of the Secretariat, but I can tell you now that we will postpone any decision, pending further developments.' He turned to the Archbishop. 'Your Grace can be assured that I will be in personal contact with you as soon as we have decided on a course of action.' He nodded politely to the others. 'Now, if you will excuse me, I would like to speak privately with Father Michel.'

Father Sykes opened the drawing-room doors and ushered the others out. Monsignor Giobbi, passing by, murmured that he would wait for me. Father Sykes was the last to leave, closing the double doors behind him. Now I was alone with the Cardinal who sat down on the sofa. 'Sit beside me, Father, this is my good side.'

Again he chafed his hands and stretched them towards the fire. 'Jeannot,' he said. 'That's what they call him, isn't it? He is small, like me. And not very robust, I am told?'

'His health seems frail, yes, Eminence.'

'And the people love him. Tell me. Do you think he will succeed?'

'I don't know. He faces enormous problems. As you know, the country is desperately poor.'

'That is true. But my question is: will he succeed in forming what the Archbishop calls a "schismatic" church?'

'With respect, Eminence, the Archbishop is not *au courant* with the true situation. As I said earlier, Father Cantave has no intention of setting up a schismatic church.'

'Martin Luther had no idea that he was setting up a schismatic church when he protested against certain of the Pope's decrees. Your friend Father Cantave may be unaware of the danger of his actions. *We* are not. Monsignor Pecci, who you met this morning, informs me that the people of Ganae—the poor—see "Jeannot" not only as their priest, but as a sort of

Redeemer. The people believe that God miraculously pro-
tects him from assassins' bullets and other dangers. Do you
know anything of this?'

'It's true,' I said. 'But Father Cantave has nothing to do
with such talk. He would certainly try to discourage it.'

'Are you sure? We hear otherwise.'

I was angry and it showed in my answer. 'Well, it's simply
not true, Eminence.'

'Good.' He paused, then, surprisingly, took my hand, holding it between his hands as though he were about to entreat
me. 'Let me explain. I know that Father Cantave and others
like him sincerely believe that by improving the lot of the
poor they are doing God's work. They also believe that Rome
is hostile to change, that here in the Vatican we do not understand the modern world. They are wrong. We understand the
world, as it was, as it is, and as it may become. We know that
the Church is changing and will change. But if, by following
the preachings of Father Cantave, the people of Ganae lose
the Kingdom of God in the course of improving their lot here
on earth, then you and I must remember our duty. Our duty,
and Father Cantave's duty, is to remember always that, while
it is a holy and wholesome thought to wish to improve the
material lives of the poor, the primary task of the Church is,
and has always been, to save their immortal souls. In this day
and age, that task may not be uppermost in the minds of
clerics such as Father Cantave. Sincere as he may be, he is
still mortal, frail, capable of falling into heresy and leading his
people away from the true faith.

'Now, Father. After hearing what you had to say this
morning I would like to enlist your help. I want you to assure
Father Cantave that we wish him success in what he has set
out to do. It would please us, were the conditions right, to
give full and enthusiastic support to his government. Under
the rules of canon law that I spoke of earlier, we may even
decide that it is possible for him to remain a priest while he

acts as president of his country. In return, we propose certain conditions. He must cease to advocate any form of revolution. He must make peace with the Archbishop and those clergy who are not his followers. He was elected to bring democracy to Ganae. Let him work to effect that transition in a democratic manner.'

He paused and stared into the fire. 'And lastly, he must beware of the people's belief in him as a so-called Redeemer. I find that alarming. Don't you?'

'Yes, Eminence.'

'Originally, I decided that Father Cantave should not be told of this meeting. But, now that I have met you, I have changed my mind. I want you to tell Father Cantave that I have said these things to you in strictest confidence—and in the belief that, together, you and I, and he, can resolve this matter.'

'Yes, Eminence.'

'Good. Please telephone me when you return to Ganae and tell me his reaction to what I have said. The truth, mind you.'

'Yes, Eminence.'

He rose, letting go of my hand. 'Thank you, Father. Remember, I am counting on you.'

Monsignor Giobbi was waiting in the corridor. I now knew that he was my friend. He did not ask what took place in my talk with the Cardinal but enquired if I was ready to return to the residence. I thanked him for his words of support. As we walked back down the corridor he looked up at the portraits of cardinals that lined the walls. 'Some of these men were saints,' he said. 'Some were libertines. Hard to tell from their faces, isn't it?' He smiled. 'What are your plans now, Father?'

'I must fly back to Ganae at once.'

SIX

'FATHER MICHEL?'

As I crossed the tarmac in New York to board the plane that would take me on the last leg of my journey back to Ganae, Elie Audran moved alongside me, a slim, elegant figure in a beige silk suit. 'I have been following you,' he said. 'You came from Rome. I know, because I boarded your plane when it stopped over in Paris. But I was in first class, so we didn't meet. How was Rome? Cold?'

'Not very.'

'Paris was miserable. But I saw a wonderful show of *Les Fauves* at the Grand Palais, which made it worth the trip.'

I knew that whatever Elie was doing in Paris it was not simply looking at paintings. Paris was the present home of General Macandal. Elie's wife was Macandal's niece. I consoled myself that this conversation would end as soon as we boarded the plane, for, as he had pointed out, we travelled in different classes.

When Elie Audran first introduced himself to me some years before, it was as a parent asking if I could find a place in the college for his ten-year-old son who, until then, had been an indifferent scholar. A year later, after we had improved the boy's scholastic performance, Elie abruptly transferred him to an exclusive private school in Paris. The college was merely a stepping stone towards the ideal he had set for his son: to be a member of the mulatto elite.

It would not be easy. Elie had a mulatto mother but was the son of a humble black policeman. He was, he told me, a 'businessman.' One of his businesses that I knew about was canvassing for cast-off clothing from charity organisations in the United States then selling it to the poor in Port Riche. His more publicised business was as an art dealer, specialising in local primitives. His most important business connection was, of course, his connection to Macandal.

As we went up the gangway leading to the plane entrance, Elie smiled and put his hand on my shoulder. 'How is Jeannot, Father? I hear he's out of favour in Rome. True?'

'I don't think so.'

He laughed. 'Ah, well. You would know these things.'

The stewardess took our tickets and guided him to a first-class seat. 'See you at the other end, Father. Can I give you a lift into town?'

'Thank you, no. Someone's meeting me.'

I took my seat at the rear of the plane. Although we were just taking off from New York, I was already back in Ganae. I remembered the Police de Sécurité who had checked my tickets on leaving. I had said that Montreal was my final destination. But I had gone on to Rome. Would Jeannot, surrounded as he was by intrigues, wonder if I had lied to him? And now I was returning on a plane with Macandal's relative, who had offered me a lift in from the airport. I told myself that I was being foolish. Jeannot would never doubt my word. But when we landed in Port Riche, I found myself hanging back, avoiding Elie until he had collected his baggage and cleared customs.

Then, as I stood at the passport desk, Elie appeared in

front of me. 'Excuse me, Father, but I wonder if you noticed? Was I carrying a camera when we got on the plane?'

'I don't think so.'

'Damn! I must have left it in my hotel in New York. It's gone for ever now.'

At that point I was next in the queue at the passport desk. 'You're together?' the policeman said.

'No,' I said.

Elie moved away. The policeman examined my passport, stamped it and handed it back. At that point Ti-Louis, a boy from Jeannot's orphanage, who hung around the airport, came up to me. 'Want a taxi, *Mon Pe?*'

I shook my head. Normally, Ti-Louis would not have asked me. I am not someone who would require his services. I thought at once: He saw me talking with Elie. Jeannot will hear of this.

As I walked out of the terminal, carrying my bag, I saw Elie standing on the pavement about fifty yards away. He was with two soldiers. Suddenly, one of them took him by the arm and pushed him towards a parked army truck. There were six armed soldiers sitting in the truck. They dropped the tail-board and forced Elie to climb aboard. As he did he looked back, saw me, and raised his arms in a gesture of hopelessness. The truck drove away.

I turned and walked towards the airport car-park where Hyppolite was to meet me. He was standing beside our little white Peugeot, a tall, melancholy figure wearing one of my cast-off shirts and a pair of khaki trousers which once belonged to Father Joliette. He hurried to take my bag, almost wrenching it from my grip in his eagerness to help.

'*Mère ben?*' he asked, as he put the suitcase into the trunk.

I told him my mother was dead. He accepted this news with a nod. He felt no need to offer his sympathy. It was understood. We drove out on to the Avenue des Présidents in a mass of traffic: old trucks top-heavy with industrial containers stencilled with American markings, gaudily painted local taxi-buses loaded with passengers and, walking on the rim of the dusty avenue, women balancing heavy loads on their heads on the long march from the countryside to the city's markets. Abruptly, as though there were no traffic ahead of it, a large Mercedes swept past, repeatedly sounding its horn. Hyppolite looked at it as though it reminded him of something, then said, '*Madame Lambert arrête, hier.*'

I watched the limousine disappear among humbler vehicles. Caroline Lambert rode in Mercedes limousines, lived in a mansion staffed by thirty servants, sailed the Baie des Saints in a sixty-foot yacht. Caroline Lambert's cars, clothes, jewels, were the symbols of her husband's power. In Ganae a colonel in the Army earns less than a sergeant in the army of the United States. But the colonel who becomes King Coke is another matter.

Elie Audran, Caroline Lambert. The attack on the elite had begun. I looked at Hyppolite. 'What do people say?'

'They say it is time to start the justice. Start with her, that's good. Everybody know Caroline. King Coke run away, he's scared of Jeannot. But Caroline not scared. She thinks she's still boss of us. Now, we teach her.'

I looked at him, surprised. If people like Hyppolite, the silent, the humble, the submissive, those on whose mute fatalism dictators thrive, if *they* were angry, then these trials, promised by Jeannot, would be the tumbrels of vengeance.

Everybody know Caroline, Hyppolite had said. The week after her husband fled the country, Caroline Lambert's picture had appeared in magazines and newspapers both in Ganae and abroad. I discovered that she was already familiar to the people of Ganae much as a film star would be in other lands. Even those who had never seen her photograph and the hundreds and thousands who could not read a newspaper knew her story. It had been passed on by word of mouth from Port Riche into every remote hamlet, much as such things were told in medieval times. She had become the visible symbol of her husband's crimes, a beautiful, evil *mulâtre* witch, living out the fairy-tale people believed to be her life.

We turned off the Avenue des Présidents and entered the heart of the city. Here, criss-crossing like the lanes in a gigantic marketplace, were crowded thoroughfares crammed with cheap shops, open-air stalls, and peasants sitting on worn blankets, their few tawdry wares spread out at their feet. In the clamour of honking horns, street music and shouting vendors, our car slowed to five miles an hour to avoid the heedless pedestrians who danced across the street as though it were a ballroom floor. And now I saw, proliferating everywhere, the posters and proclamations which had been used in Jeannot's recent campaign for president. In former times, portraits of the dictator were put up by order of the government. Jeannot's portraits and proclamations had been erected by the poor. On crumbling walls, graffiti announced that Ganae was free at last, that: 'PE JEANNOT WILL BRING US JUSTICE.' *Pe* Jeannot. Father Jeannot. He was still their priest.

We drove on, climbing into the hills that ring the capital. In the suburbs of Bellevue the villas of the elite sat in tree-shaded grounds, surrounded by high walls and electronic alarms. There were no portraits of Jeannot on these walls. As we drove on I sensed an air of tension. In Avenue Delisle we came upon people standing in a group, staring at some sort of bonfire. Two policemen appeared in front of our car, signalling us to move past the charred and stinking remains of a heap of burning rubbish. As we did, I saw a hand-scrawled banner lying in the gutter. It read: 'BAS LE PAPE.'

'BAS LE PAPE.' Down with the Pope. We drove on. When we reached the residence, Father Denis Joliette was standing on the first-floor veranda, looking out. He waved and came down to meet me. I told him about the banner and the bonfire. 'What's happening, Denis?'

'Was it on Avenue Delisle?'

'Yes.'

'Then it's part of the anti-Rome riot.'

'What riot?'

He sighed. 'Yesterday, Jeannot went on national radio to announce that the Vatican has refused to recognise his government.'

'But that's not true. I've just been in Rome.'

He looked at me, surprised, then said, 'Anyway, this morning a mob went up to Bellevue and broke into the nuncio's house. The nuncio's in Rome but the mob didn't know that. They beat up some of the house servants, for refusing to tell them where the nuncio was hiding. They then ransacked the residence, breaking windows and smashing furniture. When they finished they lit a bonfire in the street. That must be what you saw.'

'But what about the police?'

'They just stood by. They did nothing.'

'And what has Jeannot said about this?'

Father Joliette shrugged. 'Radio silence. He put them up to it, I'll bet.'

'He wouldn't do that.'

'Of course he would. What do you think his radio speeches are all about? They're incitements to violence.'

'I know what you mean,' I said. 'But I don't think he sees them as that.'

'Paul, it's obvious you think he's a saint. He's not. He's become a rabble-rouser, a fanatic.'

'Fanatic?' I said. 'Fanatic about what? About helping the poor?'

'About getting his own way. And, as Diderot once said, "Only one step separates fanaticism from barbarism." This morning's the proof.'

He looked at me. 'By the way, what were you doing in Rome?'

'It's a long story. Denis, I've got to get in touch with Jeannot.'

While we were speaking Noël Destouts came into the room and sat down on a rocking chair near the window, lifting the skirts of his soutane to cross his legs, his large black feet clad incongruously in cheap red Cuban sandals. Noël was bursar of the college, a Ganaen, a professor of French literature, and my friend. In the past he had also been Jeannot's friend but now I wondered if he had gone over to Denis Joliette's opinions. When I said I must get in touch with Jeannot, Noël got up from the rocking chair.

'I'll drive you there,' he said. 'Jeannot's gone down to Lavallie for some sort of publicity stunt. I spoke with him an hour ago. He rang here, asking for you.'

Lavallie is the market in the dock area. It was one of the first sights tourists saw when they got off the American cruise ships for a day in Port Riche. It had always been an unpleasant, noisome maze of tin sheds and rickety stalls, its streets strewn with rotting fruit and vegetable waste, its walls slimed with mud, its corrugated iron roofs red with rust. That morning when we drove there we were obliged to leave our car several streets away. A huge crowd filled the market, most of them armed with brooms fashioned from twigs, plastic buckets, rag mops and wooden baskets. A dozen empty army trucks were lined up along the main thoroughfare. Soldiers, beggars, peasants, market sellers, nuns, schoolboys, all were engaged in cleaning off the streets, washing down walls, and carting away the detritus of decades. People sang as they worked. The music of two Java bands boomed out from the central square. I saw Jeannot, his white peasant shirt and cotton trousers already splotched with mud and grime, leading a group of his office staff in lifting wooden baskets of trash on to an army truck. The cameras of the national television station, the announcers from Radio Libre and a crush of foreign photographers moved ahead of him, elbowing each other for the best shot of the priest-president shovelling rubbish.

'What's this all about?' I asked Noël.

'It's symbolic,' Noël said. 'Clean up the streets. You start with that and end up by chasing the money changers out of the temple.'

'It looks real,' I said. 'Aren't you in favour of clean streets?'

'It's still symbolic,' Noël said. 'Will this place be clean a month from now? Will anything have changed except for Jeannot's image?'

'Wait a minute. When did the people of Lavallie clean up the streets for Doumergue, or any other president?'

But Noël didn't want an argument. He put his arm around my shoulders. 'All right,' he said. 'Will I get us a couple of brooms?'

'Why not?'

But as we went towards the crowd of sweepers, Pelardy, who was standing near the photographers, saw me and called out. 'Father Paul? Jeannot wants to see you.'

Jeannot, still handing up buckets of rubbish, paused when he saw me approach. He put down his bucket and came over. 'How is the weather in Rome?' he said.

'Jeannot, I have to tell you about that. When can we talk?'

He reached into his dirt-smeared trousers and took out the gold pocket watch I had given him as an ordination present. 'We're going to bring food in at noon. Can you wait till then?'

'Of course.'

He went back to the photographers and television crews. 'No, no, it's nationwide,' I heard him tell them. 'I've made a radio appeal for the same sort of clean up in Doumergueville, Mele and Papanos.'

I moved back to Noël who handed me a broom. 'What does our leader say?' he asked.

'I'll tell you at noon.'

Half an hour later, army trucks arrived bringing more of Jeannot's helpers, this time nuns and schoolgirls who began to set up tables laden with bowls of beans and rice. The clean-up stopped. The photographers got into their cars. The television crew began to pack up its gear. I saw Jeannot, smiling, embracing people, and being embraced. As always, the city's poor crowded around him, touching him, praising him, asking favours, giving advice. I thought of that Vatican drawing room, the fire burning in the grate, my hands being held by an old cardinal with shoulder-length silver hair. *If by following the preachings of Father Cantave, the people of Ganae lose the Kingdom of God, then you and I must remember our duty.*

But what was my duty on that morning when Jeannot's clean-up began? I watched him, his clothes dirty, his manner, as always, simple and direct, the people around him depending on him, believing in him, grateful for what he had done and was trying to do for them. Surely he was of the Kingdom of God as I could never hope to be? What *was* my duty? Was it, as the Cardinal said, to save these people's immortal souls, or was it to help Jeannot relieve their mortal misery? And as I stood there with Noël, seeing the happiness in the faces of those who crowded around the tables to eat the simple food prepared for them, into my mind came that quiet but deadly sentence: *There is no other life.*

Now, suddenly, Jeannot was in front of me. He was alone. Pelardy and other members of his staff had kept back those people who were trying to speak to him. He pointed to a huge Mercedes that sat among the army vehicles. 'Let's go to the car,' he said. 'I'll see that we're not disturbed.'

And so I sat with him in the back seat of the Mercedes which had once been the official limousine of the dictator. Six soldiers ringed the vehicle, keeping back the crowds who gathered to peer at, and wave to, their priest-president.

'How is your mother?'

I told him. He bowed his head. 'So it was true.'

'What do you mean?'

'At first, when I heard you were in Rome, I thought you'd lied to me about that.'

'I didn't lie to you. I didn't know I was to go to Rome until after my mother's funeral.'

'Why didn't you telephone me?'

'Our Provincial asked me not to.'

'And you obeyed him?'

'Yes.'

He looked at me. 'Whose side are you on, Paul?'

'Yours.'

'Are you? You came back on a plane with Elie Audran. He was in Paris, reporting to Macandal and Lambert. You were seen talking to him at the airport this morning. Very friendly. How do you know Audran?'

'For God's sake,' I said. 'His son was a pupil of mine.'

He lay back on the seat cushions. The interior of the limousine was stiflingly hot. I saw that he was trembling and sweating. I leaned over and opened the windows.

'What happened in Rome?'

I told him. I told him all of it. As I spoke, the Java bands were playing in the square. People were singing. The soldiers guarding our limousine laughed and joked among themselves, turning now and then to look shyly in at Jeannot. When I had finished, Jeannot said, 'Get in line, that's the message, isn't it? Do as we say or we'll disown you.'

'Wait. Innocenti's not asking you to abandon your principles. He's asking you to try to bring about change in a democratic manner. Arresting the likes of Caroline Lambert, and wrecking the nuncio's residence makes you look like a loose cannon.'

'I had nothing to do with the demonstration against the nuncio.'

'Nonsense. You went on radio saying the Vatican has refused to recognise your government.'

'Well, it's true, isn't it?'

'I told you. It's not true. That speech is exactly what Pellerat wanted you to say. Don't you see? You've played into the hands of your enemies.'

He stared at me.

'Pellerat wants Rome to turn against you, to excommunicate you. Listen, *Petit*. The elite is hoping you'll make a fool of yourself. Why didn't the police stop that mob? Why did they stand by and let them wreck the nuncio's residence?'

He was silent. Then he said, 'My God. Why didn't I see it?'

'You see it now. Do something. Go on the radio. Don't let them get away with it.'

He put his hand on my arm. 'You're right. I must.'

I looked up. Pelardy was approaching. Jeannot saw him too. 'Paul, what will you tell Rome?'

'What would you want me to say?'

'Buy me time. I need it.'

'I'll try.'

On that same afternoon Archbishop Pellerat, speaking at the head of the Ganaen hierarchy, apologised in a nationwide radio speech to the absent papal nuncio for what he termed was 'a disgraceful attack on the nunciature by the followers of Father Jean-Paul Cantave, an attack, inspired by President Cantave's hostility to Rome and the Holy Father.' He said it was an insult to the Holy Father that the new president of Ganae had not seen fit to issue an apology for these actions and it was the duty of every Catholic to repudiate such behaviour and the man responsible for it.

I heard the speech. I, at once, tried to reach Jeannot at the palace. I was told that he was at Radio Libre and would shortly go on the air. I called Noël Destouts into the study and we switched on the radio. Java music was playing. Halfway through the record, the sound stopped. There was si-

lence on the air and then a voice said, 'The President of
Ganae, Father Jean-Paul Cantave, will speak. Hold on.' The
music resumed and was again interrupted. 'The President,
Father Jean-Paul Cantave, will speak. Hold on.'

There was a background noise as though people were
speaking out of range of the microphone. And then silence.
Suddenly, we heard Jeannot's voice.

Brothers and Sisters,
All my Brothers and Sisters in the good Lord,
Alone we are weak.
Together we are strong.
Étienne Pellerat, Archbishop of Port Riche,
Let me look you in the eye.
I have come to tell you I love you.
Because I love you, I must tell the truth.
Truth and love are the same.

Yesterday some of our youth went to the house
Of the Pope's man in Ganae.
Their anger was just,
But their action was wrong.
The Pope's man in Ganae is not our enemy.
We must respect him.
I tell him now that we love him.
If he returns to Ganae we will honour and protect him.
For he is the Pope's man
And we are the people of the Pope.
But, Brothers and Sisters, we must not forget
Some in Ganae are not the priests of the Pope.
They are the priests of the rich,
They are the friends of our enemies.
Our enemies are vampires.
They lie in their coffins waiting to arise again
And again to drink the people's blood.

That was in the past, Brothers and Sisters,
But they will do it again.
Some of them have fled with stolen fortunes
But they want to return.
They had power,
To these vampires, power is like blood.
They will kill to get it.
We must keep our power.
We must act now.
Caroline Lambert was rich, thanks to the poor.
In a country that is poor, thanks to the rich.
You, Brothers and Sisters, have asked for justice.
I promise you that justice.
In the name of Jesus who has given us our power.
Amen.

There was silence on the airwaves. And then, suddenly, voices shouted. 'Jeann-ot! Jeann-ot!'

The national anthem blared. Noël switched it off. 'Why does he always wind up sounding violent, even when he's making a sort of apology?'

'He has enemies,' I said. 'We don't. We haven't been shot at, forced into hiding, our church burned down, our parishioners killed.'

'I didn't say he wasn't sincere. The most dangerous thing about Jeannot is that he is. And the people who surround him are sincere. But their ideas of how to change things are as dead as the Soviet Union. Liberation theology is out of date. This is a capitalist world and we have to live in it.' Noël looked at his watch. 'I must go. I have a study group at six-thirty.'

When Noël left I sat by the window as sunset darkened the roofs of a nearby slum. This wasn't 'liberation theology.' This was a faith built around one man. Listening to Jeannot speak, it had come to me that this must be how people once heard the voice of Jesus, the voice of an obscure agitator in a remote province of the Roman empire denouncing the sins of the rich and preaching the Kingdom of God. The poor of Ganae believed in Jeannot as their Messiah, a Jesus come amongst them. The Kingdom of God is founded on faith. Faith is reason's opposite. Jeannot believed that God had chosen him. Now he would use that belief to change the lives of others. At that moment I was besieged by doubts. But I had faith in him. And so, I hoped to change things.

For two weeks after our meeting Jeannot did not get in touch with me. I hesitated to call. I had nothing to report. I had done as he asked. Rome had been informed that our talks had gone well. And then, one morning while I was in class, a servant knocked on the door and told me I was wanted urgently in the school parlour.

Something about his manner alerted me. 'Who is it?'

'A gentleman. He didn't say, sir.'

The school parlour is a hot dusty room, its windows shuttered against the sun, its rattan furniture worn by years of use. It is a place where parents come to talk to their sons during school hours. When I went there that morning the room seemed empty. And then, as though he had been hiding, a man who had been standing behind the opened door came out into the slatted sunlight. He wore an open-necked shirt and trousers and at first I did not recognise him. But when he spoke, I remembered him. Colonel Maurras of the Garde Présidentielle who shot the boy, Daniel, at the gates of the palace. In the few years since I had seen him his hair had become grey, his face lined, his body coarse and thickening. He inhaled on a cigarette, coughed, and put it out.

'Do you remember me, Father?'

'Yes, Colonel.'

When I said that he went to the door and closed it, shutting us in.

'First, let me say that if you are questioned about my coming here tell them I came to ask if you will admit my nephew to your school.'

'You are still in the Army?'

He nodded. 'After the shooting I asked for a transfer to Doumergueville. I tried to forget what happened. But, of course, that wasn't possible. That's why I came today. I am not brave, Father. But I remember what Father Cantave said to me that morning. I feel I owe it to him to warn you that he is in great danger.'

Again, he looked at the closed door. 'We will not be interrupted?'

'I doubt it.'

I pointed to a chair, but he shook his head and walked to the window, peering out through the shutters. In the distance I heard singing as the school choir began to practise a hymn. He turned back to me and spoke in a low voice, his words jumbling into each other.

'I don't know details, so don't ask me, and you must tell Father Cantave that if he brings me in for questioning he is signing my death warrant and perhaps his own. There are those who are planning a coup. I can't tell you when it will happen, but it will not be until after the parliamentary elections in April. What happens at the elections will be the excuse. The Army doesn't want it to look like a military coup. If the Army deposes Father Cantave and forms a junta there will be international protest. So the idea is to put some other politician in power. Don't ask me who, I don't know his name. I can tell you this. The coup is being planned in Paris. Lambert's at the head of it. When it happens, General Macandal will fly back to Ganae and take over the Army. General Hemon, who is backing Father Cantave, will be offered exile. Lambert believes that when Hemon realises the situation he will co-operate.'

He stopped speaking and pulled out a pack of cigarettes. 'I

have been asked to take a small group of soldiers to the palace on the morning of the coup. I know the procedures to gain entry. We will arrest and hold Father Cantave. As we do this, the politician I have told you about will be driven to Radio Libre to make a broadcast. He will announce that Father Cantave has been replaced as president because of his refusal to co-operate with parliament and govern by democratic methods. When we hear the broadcast begin, we, at the palace, will shoot Father Cantave.' He paused and nervously lit a fresh cigarette. 'When they asked me to join the coup they believed I was Doumergue's man. They didn't guess that I cannot kill Father Cantave. I cannot kill a saint, although he is a saint who does not know how to govern this country and his rule will not last. I don't know what you will do now, or how you can advise him. He must change his guard at the palace. It should be a guard of soldiers who are his followers. But this is the most important part, Father, and this is what you must tell him. He must pretend to know nothing of this plan. If he does, I promise you I will tell you the date and the time as soon as I find out. So when we arrive at the palace he will have gone into hiding. Will you tell him that?'

'Yes.'

'I may be followed here today. They are being very careful. We must have a code, you and I. The simplest thing would be for me to come here to the college and leave a message if I do not reach you. The message will say that I want to bring my nephew to see you and I will propose a date. That date will be the date of the coup.'

Then this strange man came up to me, gripped me by the shoulders and stared into my face. 'Do as I say, Father, and he will be saved. But you must warn him. If he attempts to arrest me or to contact me in any way, they will kill me. I am putting my life in his hands. And in yours.'

Still holding me, he pressed his sweating cheek against mine. Then, releasing me, he opened the door and, with no farewell, walked off down the corridor to the school's main entrance. An army jeep was parked by the front door. I watched him get in and drive away.

That evening at six when my school duties were completed and my absence would not be noticed, I left the residence and drove to the palace. I did not telephone ahead. When I was admitted to the main hall I asked for Pelardy but, instead, was greeted by Sister Maria. 'Father Cantave is ill,' she told me. 'Is it urgent?'

When I said yes, she asked me to wait. I noticed that there were several young soldiers standing by the entrance, armed with automatic pistols and bearing a shoulder flash which I had not seen before. The Garde Présidentielle had been in evidence at the main gates but when Sister Maria came back and led me up flights of marble stairs, along panelled corridors and again up more stairs, I saw small groups of these young soldiers at every turn. On the top floor of the palace, we went towards a wing that jutted out over the main square. The usual presidential bodyguards, those heavy-set sergeants, were nowhere in sight. Instead, two young soldiers opened a double set of doors to admit us to a huge bedroom dominated by a tall four-poster bed, a room which could have been a royal bedroom in some European palace. There were many chairs grouped around the bed, all of them empty.

The room was hot. The great windows that looked out over the presidential square and the rooftops of the parliament buildings were closed and covered by screens. There was a smell of medicine and rubbing alcohol. The bed itself was surrounded by mosquito netting. As I came closer I saw Jeannot, wearing a long white nightshirt, propped up among many pillows. Above him, a simple wooden crucifix was nailed to the headboard. At his side were two telephones and his breviary. A mass of official-looking files was strewn about the bed. He appeared to be asleep, but when Sister Maria left the room he opened his eyes and smiled at me.

'Ridiculous, isn't it, this bed. Yet, there's a lot of history in this room. Did you know this is the bed Doumergue died in? Screaming, they say. Seydoux, who was president in the twenties, was shot to death at that window. They came for President Mouton in the middle of the night. He hid under this bed and they dragged him out and cut his throat. That was in the nineteenth century. He was *noir*, like me. Then there was President Beauvais, in the eighteen-nineties, the one whose carriage was called the virgin's hearse. He brought them to bed here. Thirteen-year-old girls, mostly.'

'And now there's a breviary in the bed.'

'True.' He laughed. 'How are you, Paul? Where have you been?'

'Are you ill, Jeannot?'

'It's nothing. A little fever. I feel cold all the time. What's wrong? You have that familiar worried look.'

I pulled aside the mosquito netting and sat on the edge of his bed. When I began to tell him what had happened that morning he sat up with his hand over his eyes, a gesture which signalled that he was fighting off a migraine. When I finished, he nodded and said, 'Strange that it would be you who would find out. I've been expecting this. You know about Raymond?'

Alphonse Raymond was the head of the Progressive Party which ran a poor second to Jeannot in the elections.

'What about him?'

'Parliament wants to make him our premier. I've refused. I want my premier to be someone from my own group. So they're calling me a dictator. Raymond must be the one they've picked to replace me as president.'

'But that's parliament,' I said. 'This colonel is talking of a military coup.'

'It's one and the same thing,' Jeannot said. 'They're all in it together, the parties, the generals, the businessmen, the elite.

I have only one strength and I'll have to use it. The people. We must show our fist.'

'What do you mean?'

'You'll see. As for having my own guards, I've already thought of that. Did you notice my hand-picked soldiers?'

'Yes. Who are they?'

'They're not real soldiers. They're my own *bleus*, boys who were once in the Ste Marie Orphanage. Because, as your colonel pointed out, we can no longer trust anyone in the real army. The question is—can we trust your colonel?'

'Why shouldn't we?'

'We're supposed to relax until he tells us the coup is under way. If he's a plant, then we're being lulled into a false sense of security.'

He reached up and gripped my hand. 'Paul, thank you for coming. Don't stay away. Come every day, if you can. This is our moment of truth.'

SEVEN

I N GANAE television is perceived as an instrument of government. And so the event which occurred one week after I spoke to Jeannot may have been planned and staged by his staff. For, on the following Monday morning, the daily sludge of canned musical programmes was interrupted by a seemingly unscheduled telecast, a look at the city of Port Riche in what seemed to be the first stages of a revolution.

There was a large television set in the main dining hall of the college. I don't know who had turned it on. But, shortly before lunchtime, the college servants, setting out cutlery for the midday meal, were suddenly aware of what was happening. Within minutes, classes had been interrupted and priests, students, and everyone else crowded into the big room, watching in amazement.

We were looking at the Avenue Beaucaire, a main thoroughfare leading up to the parliament buildings. A mass of people holding aloft placards with makeshift banners and the now familiar portrait of Jeannot was moving in a great chanting flood, filling the street, crowding against the adjoining buildings. The television crews, unskilled in spontaneous filming, moved erratically ahead of the demonstrators, cameras tilting upwards to catch glimpses of the banners' hand-printed slogans.

JEANNOT IS US—RAYMOND IS THEM
POWER TO THE POOR
JEANNOT
OUR VOICE—DON'T SHUT HIM OUT

As we watched, the procession approached the gates of the parliament buildings. Inside the courtyard the cars of parliamentary delegates could be seen parked in rows, a sign that parliament was in session. In front of the gates soldiers were disembarking from trucks and hastily shuffling into a double line to block the demonstrators. At the head of the crowd I saw four young priests wearing white soutanes, two of them holding aloft processional crucifixes, and two presenting open pages of bibles, as though bearing witness. Behind them were the familiar faces of Port Riche's lower town, women in white bandannas and ugly flowered dresses, grey-grizzled, rheumy-eyed old men, thin starveling girls in short white shifts, nervous, stick-like little boys. The television cameras, rising higher, showed the thick mass of the crowd behind these emblematic representatives of the slums. Suddenly, the voice of a commentator was heard.

'We are at the Place du Parlement where a march led by supporters of President Cantave has come to protest parliament's proposal to appoint the leader of the Progressive Party, Alphonse Raymond, as premier of Ganae. Father Cantave's choice, Yves Gabin, has been rejected by parliament on the grounds that he has close ties to the President and this, in effect, encourages one-party rule. As you can see, this demonstration is made up of ordinary people, most of them belonging to the poorer classes. The crowd is calling for Members of Parliament to appear and answer its chal-

lenge, but it now seems unlikely that they will receive the
courtesy of a reply.'

At that point, the commentator seemed to run out of
words. The cameras roved aimlessly over the heads of the
crowd. When, at last, they came to rest on the rows of
soldiers lined up at the parliament gates, the commentator
found his voice again. 'It is obvious that the Army, under the
command of General Hemon, is backing the President and
these soldiers are here purely to maintain order. Violence is
being avoided.'

And, indeed, there was no violence. After a few minutes the
huge crowd, as if on orders, began to move away from the
parliament buildings, going back up the Avenue Beaucaire in
straggling, disorderly fashion as though the demonstration
were breaking up. At that point the television cameras were
shut off and the television screen showed a studio interior. An
announcer, sitting at a desk, told us we were now being returned to normal programming.

'This is an historic occasion,' Father Duchamp said as we
ate our lunch. 'Dictators put down demonstrations. Jeannot
provokes them. The mob is his army.'

Duchamp was, of course, in the habit of making this type of
sarcastic comment and normally I would have tried to ignore
his remark. But, on that same afternoon, Monsignor Taburly,
the Vatican's acting chargé d'affaires in Ganae, asked me to
come and see him on an urgent matter which he could not
discuss on the phone.

I went at once.

Driving through the city on my way to Bellevue, I noticed
that the daily street market had disappeared from the pavements of the Rue Royale and that shops were shuttered as on
a Sunday. On Rue Desmoulins my car was stopped by a
crowd of boys standing by a threatening pile of stones. Three
of them came up to me, rocks poised in their hands.

'Do you have cigarettes?' one asked.

'Let me through.'

They stared at me for a moment. Then one of them recognised me. '*Pe Paul, Pe Paul. Ami.*'

So they were Jeannot's boys. They smiled foolishly, like children caught in some prank. They waved me on. But when I looked back they had stopped another car.

The nunciature still flew the papal flag on its front lawn, but was shuttered and silent as though its occupants were elsewhere. When I parked in the empty courtyard and rang the doorbell, Taburly himself opened the door for me. He was dressed oddly in white trousers, an open-necked shirt, and velvet slippers embroidered in gold with his initials. Taburly was French. I knew that he was not happy with his posting here. 'Come in, come in,' he said. 'Good of you to come so quickly.'

He led me upstairs to a large room, a sort of office, equipped with fax machines, telephones and a computer. 'I've received a query from Rome. Cardinal Innocenti is worried about the situation. I'm afraid I won't be able to reassure him. You saw the television this morning?'

'Yes.'

He went to a desk and handed me a fax. It was in Italian. 'I'm sorry,' I said. 'I don't—'

'Of course.' He took it back. 'It's from the Cardinal. He asks me to contact you and find out what you know. He says Rome has been advised that Father Cantave is about to establish a dictatorship. If this is so, he says he must reconsider the guarantees he gave you. He asks for an immediate answer.'

'From me?'

'From both of us. I will be glad to transmit your report to him. When can you send it?'

'First, I must speak with Father Cantave.'

'As you wish. I am sending my own report tonight. I will tell the Cardinal of this morning's march on parliament. In view of what's happening, I must recommend that Rome now distance itself from Cantave.'

As he spoke, a servant appeared in the doorway. Taburly turned to me. 'I've just ordered some tea. Would you care to join me?'

'Thank you, no.'

When I drove back to the college, it was late in the afternoon. Classes were over but I noticed that the study halls were empty and the reading room where students tended to congregate in their off hours was similarly deserted. 'Where is everyone?' I asked Noël Destouts.

'In the streets. Great excitements.'

'What do you mean?'

'Our friend Jeannot. Broadcasts and demonstrations. Quite disturbing.'

I went into the masters' common room and turned on both television and radio. The radio played funeral music and the television was running an American soap opera dubbed into French. I picked up the phone and rang the palace. The lines were busy. I kept redialling and after several minutes was put through to Pelardy.

'How can I reach Jeannot? Is he in the palace?'

'May I ask what it's about, Father?'

'I have news from Rome.'

'Hold on. I'll tell him.'

I waited. Another voice came on. 'The President is leaving for Radio Libre in ten minutes' time. Where are you?'

'At the college residence.'

'Hold on, please.'

After a further delay, the same voice said, 'If you will wait outside the residence, a car will pick you up in about fifteen minutes' time.'

I went down to the courtyard. It was growing dark. I could

hear the sound of a radio playing in our garage. It switched off and Hyppolite came out, asking if I wanted to take the car.

'No, no, I'm waiting for someone.'

'It's bad in the city,' Hyppolite said. 'The justice start. It start now.'

'What do you mean?'

At that moment a horn sounded urgently in the street outside. A black Mercedes had drawn up at the entrance. Ti-Tomas, one of Jeannot's self-appointed bodyguards, got out and waved to me. Mathieu Clément, Jeannot's new press secretary, sat in the front seat beside the driver. When Ti-Tomas held open the door for me, I saw Jeannot in the back seat, hunched over a walkie-talkie. He did not look at me. He was listening intently to a garbled murmur from the walkie-talkie. He leaned forward and tapped Clément on the shoulder. 'No, no. We have to go there.'

'What's wrong?' I asked.

'Trouble. We just heard it on the radio.'

As the car drove away from the residence I looked at Jeannot. His eyes were closed, his brow furrowed as though he were trying to remember or memorise something. We weaved through narrow streets and emerged in La Canebière, the boulevard that winds down towards the seafront.

'Where are we going?' I asked, for it was clear that we were not driving in the direction of Radio Libre.

No one answered. We passed under the mouldering arches of the old exhibition grounds. Ahead, on a promontory overlooking the ocean, was the grey hulk of Fort Noël, the great prison of Port Riche. Like all infamous prisons it was a place of legend, its name a register of terror. We were now in the narrow road that led to its gates. Ahead was a queue of slow-moving vehicles. At sight of them Jeannot slipped off his seat, crouching on the car floor. As we slowed to a crawl in the traffic, a siren started up behind us. A police car moved alongside, its warning lights flashing. The driver waved to Mathieu

Clément and the police car moved in front of us, leading us out of the queue to the head of the line of traffic and straight up to the forbidding walls of the prison. There, a mass of people jostled each other, holding up banners, shouting slogans, beating long sticks together to make a din. Faces peered in at us. I leaned over Jeannot, shielding him from sight. As the main prison gates opened to admit us we moved past a double line of army vehicles in which sat soldiers armed with automatic weapons. Searchlights played on the high walls, then swept down to the demonstrators. Looking back, I caught sight of a banner, waving above the crowd.

OÙ EST CAROLINE?

In the courtyard, four officers, members of the Army's general staff, saluted smartly as Jeannot stepped out of the car. A sergeant turned and ran inside the prison. Moments later, General Hemon, tall, heavily built, with close-cropped grey hair and military moustache, came out, accompanied by a thickset mulatto who was dressed in green combat fatigues and running shoes.

Jeannot looked at Mathieu Clément. 'Who?' he whispered.

'The prison governor.'

Hemon, the governor, and Jeannot then walked a few paces away from the rest of us. Jeannot said something. The General shook his head. Jeannot spoke to the prison governor who nodded and signalled to a subordinate. Hemon abruptly walked away from Jeannot and paced up and down the courtyard alone, watched by his staff officers.

Outside the prison walls the din of protest continued. I looked back at the gates and saw that two vans from the national radio and television stations had been admitted into the courtyard. The television crew was setting up its equipment. Two women guards came from the interior of the prison. Between them, her hands manacled, was Caroline

Lambert. She wore a short, grey prison dress with a convict number stencilled on her shoulder. Her long blonde hair, no longer coiffed or dyed, was streaked in its natural brown colour. She looked pale and ill, very different from the elegant person I had seen in photographs. But I was caught by her beauty. I saw her turn and look at Jeannot as though he were her executioner. Jeannot saw it too and went up to her, taking her hands in his as though she were an old and valued friend. It was a strange tableau: the grim courtyard, lit by prison searchlights; a small, youthful, black man holding the manacled hands of a tall, beautiful, mulatto girl.

'I'm sorry, Madame,' Jeannot said. 'Believe me, I've disturbed you this evening only because I must. Some foreign radio station has issued a broadcast saying that you have escaped from prison. Of course it was done maliciously to excite our people and cause civil disturbances. So, I must ask for your help.'

He turned, went over to the governor and spoke to him. The governor signalled and at once the prison gates swung open. Seeing this, the crowd outside moved up to the entrance, shouting and beating sticks. Jeannot took Caroline Lambert's arm, leading her forward as though this were some official ceremony. In the darkness, the crowd did not see Jeannot and Caroline until the prison searchlights swept down towards the interior of the courtyard.

Letting go of Caroline, Jeannot stepped into the harsh white glare. There was an instant tumult of cheering. He turned back, into the shadows, to lead Caroline into the blinding light. At once, the crowd became a huge angry animal, yelling her name, calling out obscenities, shaking fists and beating on their long sticks. The soldiers stationed just outside the gates stood up in their trucks, guns pointing at the shouting people. I saw Caroline flinch and move back into the shadows. Jeannot let her go. He moved into the centre of the

circle made by the searchlight and held up his hands for silence. The shouting died.

Brothers and Sisters,
You know this woman,
You see her before you tonight.
It is not true that she has run away.
She is in our custody.
She is the wife of King Coke.
He gave her furs and jewels, he gave her riches.
Riches he made
From the misery of the poor.
And she helped him, yes, she helped him.
That is why she is here tonight.
We have courts which are the courts of the people.
Let these courts decide her punishment.
We must be just.
I am here tonight to enforce the law.
Why?
Because Someone greater than me has given me this task.
Jesus loved the poor.
He sacrificed His life for them.
As I would sacrifice my life for you.
We must be prepared to do as He did.
To sacrifice our lives for one another,
Brothers and Sisters,
Do not be afraid.
We will come into our paradise, I promise you.
Look at this woman.
She is in our prison.
It was the prison of the dictator Doumergue,
The poor of Ganae died here.
They were tortured here,
They were shot and strangled here.
There were no trials in those days.

There was no such thing as justice.
Are we Doumerguists?

The crowd roared, 'No!'

Then go home tonight in confidence.
This woman will not escape our justice.
She will be one of many.
You will have justice, I promise you.
And now I ask you, each and every one.
I ask you all,
Wherever you are watching,
Wherever you are listening.
I ask you to tell your friends.
Let us have no riots in our streets tonight.
Let no one steal the goods of others.
We are one!
We are the people and we are together.
Bless you, Brothers and Sisters.
Now, go in peace.

He moved out of the searchlight which swivelled and fo-
cused on the crowd at the open gates. The gates closed. The
searchlight died, leaving the demonstrators in total darkness.
The beating of sticks started up sporadically and voices called,
'Jeannot! Jeannot!' but the momentum of the cries diminished.

In the darkened courtyard Jeannot turned to General
Hemon. 'Are there reports of other demonstrations?'

'It's quieting down. At least, here in Port Riche.'

'I will be in the palace tonight, if you need to reach me,'
Jeannot said. Hemon nodded and walked over to his staff car.
At this point I was standing close to Jeannot. Caroline Lambert, flanked by her jailers, turned and came up to us. To my
astonishment she spoke, not to Jeannot, but to me.

'You are Father Paul Michel?'

'Yes.'

'I don't know you, Father, but I have heard many people speak of you. Would it be possible for me to see you now, in private? That is, if the President will permit it?'

I looked at Jeannot, who said at once, 'Of course, Madame. Paul, I must get back to the palace but I'll send a car for you, so that you can join me later.'

He turned to Caroline Lambert. 'Goodnight, Madame. Again, my thanks.'

Hemon's staff car had already passed through the main gates. Jeannot's aides waited by the black Mercedes as Jeannot shook hands with the prison governor. The Mercedes drove out into the night. The gates shut and, at a signal from the governor, the women warders led us through the prison doors. Inside, I at once smelled a special stench, a mixture of excrement and strong disinfectant. I followed Caroline Lambert down ill-lit corridors, past foul cells crowded with prisoners, who, when they saw her, became excited, yelling insults and threats even more vehement than the shouts of the mob outside the prison gates. Some made sexual gestures, others mimed throat-slitting, some howled at her like animals. Walking behind her I felt as though, unloosed from their bars, they would have massacred us both. Caroline Lambert ignored the tumult, walking steadily, staring straight ahead. The wardress unlocked a heavy iron door and we passed into a large hall whose filthy dining tables had recently been hosed down, then into a narrow corridor where there were cells shut off from outside view. An old turnkey, wearing a faded black-and-red cap which I recognised as the uniform cap of the prison service in Doumergue's day, unlocked a small iron door which creaked eerily as he closed us in. I was now alone with Caroline Lambert, not in a cell but in a sort of interrogation room. There was an overhead light, a scarred wooden table and two chairs. In a corner were a pail of water and a bench on which lay a jumble of half-seen objects, including a rubber truncheon. Here, the noise of the prison was stilled. This was a room of silence.

I pulled out a chair for her and we sat facing each other. She was beautiful. As I looked at her I was filled with a strange resentment, an anger I had often felt in my youth when I realised that to young women I was a priest, something other than a male. I was ashamed of this prideful vanity and surprised that it had come back to me now, in the forty-seventh year of my life.

'What is it you want to talk about, Madame?'

She glanced at the door, as though worried that we might be overheard. When she spoke it was in the accents of the Parisian upper classes for, like many of Ganae's *gratin*, she had been educated in France. 'People have told me about you,' she said. 'Simon Lamballe says you are a good man, not political, like Father Cantave. And Artemis Brun. I know he was a bad person but when he was put in prison you gave money from your own pocket to help his wife and you kept his son in your school. There are many stories about you, you know them better than I. They say that you are the one who keeps Cantave from doing terrible things.'

'That's not true. What is it you want?'

'There is no reason you should help me.' As she spoke, she ran her fingers distractedly through her long, dark-streaked and, I now saw, dirty hair. 'I know how much I am hated. People all over my country have been told about my parties, the caviar I fed to my guests, the cases of champagne that were drunk in my house, while outside in the streets there is despair and AIDS and terrible poverty. I know that children die of hunger every day. It's true, it's true, but we have always had poverty in Ganae. Remember, Father, I didn't choose my parents. I am a member of what your friend Cantave calls the elite. It was normal for me to have good clothes, luxuries, all of that. After all, my grandfather was president of this country. I married Alain Lambert, a man of my class, an officer in the Army. No one told me about this drug thing before I married him. I didn't ask him about any of that. Never. It just wasn't done. Of course I knew that he had money, lots of it. But in my circle, it's understood that high officers in the Army have access to contracts, to all sorts of advantages. I am being punished not for what I did but for who I am. I am Alain Lambert's wife. That's my crime. And I am going to die because of it.'

'You are not going to die,' I said. 'A court might sentence your husband to death, although I doubt it. But not you.'

'How do you know? If you say that, you don't understand your friend Cantave. He sees himself as an instrument of vengeance. Now, he has incited the mob to take the law into its own hands.'

'That's not true.'

'Oh yes it is. Are you blind, Father? I am not blind. I have been two months in this place. The lawyer given me by your government assures me that I will not be sentenced to death. But I am already under sentence of death. Twice they have tried to kill me.'

'What do you mean?'

'You've seen them out there. They hate me. Look.' She tugged at the neckline of her prison dress, baring her shoulder and the upper part of her breast. A long ugly wound, red and recent, cut deep into the flesh. 'This happened last week when I was in the toilets. The prison people did not even bother to bandage it. They laughed at me. And then, four days ago, someone tripped me as I stood at the top of the stairwell. If I had not been caught and held by a *mulâtre* I would have fallen a hundred feet to my death. Afterwards the man who helped me was beaten by the other prisoners. The guards stood by, laughing. It may happen again tomorrow, it may happen next week. They are not going to wait for a trial. Do you understand, Father? They want to kill me. I have protested to the governor but he ignores me. I have written a letter to Cantave. Perhaps it never reached him. Does he want a trial, or does he want to see me killed like a dog? Ask him that.'

She reached across the table and put her manacled hands on mine. Her touch was intimate. I cannot explain it, but it was sexual, in a way I unwittingly craved. I believed her. I had just walked past those rows of cells, past those shouting, screaming faces. I looked at her and in that moment was filled with urgent, hopeless desire.

'I will help you,' I said. 'I'll speak to him at once.'

She pressed my hand tightly. Tears came into her eyes. We stared at each other for a long moment and then she withdrew her touch. She stood up. We were being watched for, as soon as she stood, I heard the door open with its eerie, ratlike squeal. The old turnkey stood in the open doorway touching his cap. 'Finish, *Mon Pe?*'

'Yes.'

'This way, *Mon Pe.*'

We went out into the corridor. The two women warders who were waiting there moved towards Caroline and I saw that she would be led off in another direction. Caroline Lambert looked at them, hesitated, then turned to me, smiling in a parody of that social manner she must have used all her life.

'Thank you for seeing me, Father. I'm sorry to have kept you so late.'

The female warders closed in on either side of her. I watched, with ineluctable longing, until she was out of sight.

EIGHT

ABLACK MERCEDES, flying the presidential colours on its front bumper, waited for me in the prison courtyard. The uniformed chauffeur held open the door and touched his cap respectfully before taking his place behind the wheel. As we drove through darkened streets, the city seemed asleep. There were few vehicles about and no sign of police or soldiers. Yet, somewhere in the distance, I heard shouts and, as we moved through the central market area, the sky was reddened by bonfires, attended by chanting, drunk-seeming youths. The shouts and yelling diminished as we drove towards the dead-of-night torpor of the parliament buildings and, at last, the vast deserted square surrounding the silence of the palace.

I was expected. Mathieu Clément, Jeannot's press aide, waited at the main entrance and again I was led up many flights of marble stairs to the east wing and Jeannot's private quarters. Tonight, he was not in his bedroom but in a large, book-lined library, the sort of ceremonial room where heads of state sit with important foreign guests, smiling and miming conversation as photographers record the meeting.

Jeannot stood by the window, looking out into the night. When he turned round, I sensed that he was apprehensive.

'So what *is* the news from Rome?'

'Cardinal Innocenti has been getting reports that you're trying to set up a dictatorship.'

'Reports from who? From Taburly? From the Archbishop?'

'Probably from both,' I said. 'But I suspect Rome's worried because the foreign press is beginning to say dangerous things about you. You must have seen the stories in the *New York Times* and *Le Monde*. The fact that you've refused to negotiate with parliament, the fact that you want to appoint your own premier—it sounds to the outside world as if nothing has changed since the days of Doumergue. And now these demonstrations—whatever you call them—are being viewed as incitements to violence.'

'They're nothing of the sort. They're merely a warning that people have power and will use it to get their way.'

'*Their* way?' I said. 'What does that mean?'

'Justice.'

'Justice? What sort of justice is there in putting someone like Caroline Lambert on trial when the real criminals are sitting free in Paris? Or arresting the likes of Elie Audran, whose main crime seems to be that he's Macandal's brother-in-law? How many other small-fry have you locked up lately?'

'You don't understand. We're sending our enemies a message.'

'What sort of message are you sending by putting someone's wife in jail?'

'I see,' he said. 'It's Caroline Lambert. That's what's upset you, isn't it?'

I felt my face hot. 'What do you mean?'

'I might have known. She's clever, all right. She picked the right person. Good, kind Father Michel whose big heart is well known. What did she tell you? That she's a victim of paranoia? Did she throw herself on your mercy? What was it, Paul?'

'They're going to kill her,' I said. 'Any day now.'

'Who's going to kill her?'

'The people you taught to hate her. Her fellow prisoners in Fort Noël.'

'Is that what she says? It's nonsense.'

'Is it?'

He stared at me. 'Why do you believe her?'

'Why not? She's not a criminal. She's Lambert's wife, that's all she is. Don't you realise what you're doing? You've made her the scapegoat for everything that's wrong here. You saw that crowd tonight outside the prison. But you didn't see what I did, the crowd inside, the prisoners, screaming at her. They've already tried to kill her. Twice. Did you get the letter she sent you?'

'What letter?'

'*Did* you get it?'

My voice was loud. In all of our years together, Jeannot and I had never talked in this way.

For a moment he did not speak. Then he said, 'Even you. I've been told it, but I didn't believe it. She can twist any man around her little finger. Anyone.'

My anger was now so great that I couldn't answer him. Then Jeannot, with that grace he had always possessed, came to me, gripped my shoulder and said, 'Paul, I'm sorry. I shouldn't have said that. Maybe you're right. I'll ask the governor to put her under special protection.'

'That's not enough.'

'What would you suggest, then?'

'We've got to get her out of there.'

'Where would we put her?'

'I've thought of a place, a safe place. Let me find out if it's possible to send her there.'

'All right. Do it.' He turned towards the window, and

looked out at the night. Moonlight bathed the great square. 'Now let's talk about Rome,' he said. 'If Rome forces me to choose between being a priest or the President, what am I going to do? I can't make that choice because first, last, and always I see myself as a priest. Can't you make them understand? Can you reassure Cardinal Innocenti in some way?'

'I can try.'

'Please, Paul? It means—well, you know what it means to me.'

The following day I sent a facsimile report to Cardinal Innocenti. I did not send it through the nunciature because I did not want Taburly to contradict me. I told the Cardinal that Jeannot very much regretted the demonstrations and had promised to negotiate peacefully with his political rivals when the Senate elections came up in six weeks' time. When I sent that report I was, as always, loyal to Jeannot and working on his behalf. But, for the first time, we were trading with each other. If I helped him, he would help me. For—there is no other word for it—I had become obsessed with Caroline Lambert. In those few days she was constantly in my mind: the image of her sitting across from me in that sinister room, tears in her eyes, her hands touching mine.

I had a plan. I remembered a visit I had made to a convent of Carmelite nuns in a remote part of Cap Nord. I managed to get through to the Mother Superior on the telephone. When I explained my dilemma, she agreed to take Caroline Lambert in until such time as she came to trial.

That same evening I went to the presidential palace. Jeannot received me during his dinner hour. He sat at a long table with his aides, all of them eating and arguing together. First, I told him of my report to Cardinal Innocenti. He was pleased. Then I told him about the Carmelite nuns. He looked up and down the table to see if any of his aides were listening. But the group was noisily engaged in some debate about how to get rice supplies to a starving village in Mele.

Jeannot leaned towards me. 'How would she get there? It would have to be done in secret. Someone would have to take her. Who could we trust?'

'I'll take her.'

There was a silence. Then he said, 'You know I don't want to do this. You also know I can't refuse you. Tell me. The convent isn't a prison. What's to prevent her running away?'

'The convent is like a prison. It's remote, on a mountain top, approached by a dirt track, which can be travelled only on foot or by muleback. There is no village for forty miles in any direction. I've spoken to the Reverend Mother and she's promised they'll keep a very close watch on her. If, and when, you hold a trial, she will have to return to Port Riche. I know that.'

He looked at me. 'And the other, more important, matter?' he said. 'If you are not at the college, how will I be warned?'

'Remember, we've been told that it won't happen until after the elections at the end of April. Tomorrow is the 15th of March. I'll only be gone for three days, at most.'

'Still . . .'

'Look. If the Colonel shows up, Noël Destouts will take the message. Noël will be deputising for me. He's your friend. We can trust him. I'll ask him to telephone you.'

'He's my friend,' Jeannot said. 'But I don't want you to tell him what's going on. We've agreed, haven't we? We tell no one.'

And so, I did as Jeannot asked. I told Noël only that the Colonel's message, if it came, was a code for something political and that he must telephone Jeannot as soon as he received it.

'But where are *you* off to?' Noël wanted to know.

I lied. I told everyone at the college that I was going to Cap Nord because Jacques Letellier, one of my scholarship pupils, now a judge, had become seriously ill. On the day after my second meeting with Jeannot, I went to the orphanage in Laramie that was run by the Sisters of Ste Marie. There I obtained a nun's habit and sandals which I stowed into a canvas bag. Sister Dolores, a tall, heavily built Ganaen, the owner of the habit, was intensely curious as to my reason for borrowing it. I don't remember what lie I told her, but by now I had become glib at dissembling.

Shortly before dawn on the following day I drove up to the grim gates of Fort Noël. Jeannot had telephoned ahead. I was admitted at once and led to the governor's office. There, sitting on a bench, was Caroline Lambert. The governor, roused early from his bed, was drinking coffee at his desk. I handed him the letter that Jeannot had given me. He read it suspiciously, then asked, 'Where are you taking her?'

'I'm sorry. I can't say.'

I opened the canvas bag and took out the nun's habit and sandals. 'Put these on,' I told her.

The governor watched as she struggled into the oversized, old-fashioned habit.

'Pull the head-dress forward,' I said. 'Conceal your face.'

'No release form, no transfer of the prisoner,' the governor said. 'It's as though I'm letting her escape.'

He rose and looked out at the main prison courtyard.

'Is that your car down there?'

'Yes.'

'The six o'clock guard shift comes on in about ten minutes' time. If you leave quickly, I don't think anyone will notice her.'

And so, as dawn came up, a priest and a nun passed through the gates of Fort Noël and drove down to the terminal at Rue Desmoulins where decrepit public transport buses leave for the rural regions.

'Where are you taking me?'

'To a convent, far from here.'

'Not a prison?'

'No. But you must stay there for a time. I've given my word that you won't run away. I must trust you. And I'm asking you to trust me.'

She turned and looked at me directly. 'Of course I trust you.'

When we reached the bus station, Hyppolite was waiting for me outside the entrance. He did not look at the 'nun' who was with me. When I handed him the car keys, he smiled and said, '*Bon voyage, Pe Paul.*'

We watched him drive off in the car. I took her into the terminal and pointed to a bench near the ticket booths. 'Will you wait there?'

She nodded and sat, her head bent forward, her face concealed by the ample head-dress. I went to the booth and bought two tickets to Damienville, the last stop on the northern route. As I paid for the tickets I looked back at her. What would I do if she tried to run away?

When I returned with the tickets and two *beignets* which I bought from a nearby kiosk, she took the food, thanked me and ate, still hiding her face from the other passengers who ran about, shouting at each other, asking questions, searching for the right departure platform. I had to leave her again while I, too, searched. When, at last, I found the Damienville bus, I seated us in the back row, behind a mother and three small, noisy children.

The bus, half-filled, began to move out of the terminal, its ancient engine noisily backfiring as we rolled into the Rue Desmoulins. One of the children, a little girl not more than five years old, put her head over the back of the seat, staring at us. After a moment she put her index fingers into her ears, wiggling them in performance for our benefit. Caroline Lambert laughed. The child, delighted, disappeared from view. And then Caroline, turning to me, put her hand on mine.

'Thank you for saving my life.'

Her hand, holding mine. My hand, pressing hers, returning the secret embrace in a contact intimate as the touch of no other person in my life. I did not speak, nor did she. The ancient bus rumbled through the centre of the city, anonymous, unnoticed, a busload of poor folk—factory workers, farm labourers, artisans who had come to the city to offer their wares. I was alone with her, her body close. I trembled in strange exaltation.

In Ganae, as in no other country, to leave the slums of the capital is to enter an alternate scene of misery, the desolation of a land denuded of its trees, its fields debilitated by ignorant plantings of crop upon crop, its peasants living in lean-to shacks which give little shelter from the unrelenting sun and drenching rains. All day long, our bus travelled dusty roads, climbing into the harsh mountains, stopping in small villages, usually on the banks of a stream, where large-eyed children, their bodies brittle from undernourishment, clustered around the embarking or descending travellers in a listless charade of begging for coins. And then in late afternoon, as we came within twenty miles of Damienville, a man climbed on to the bus, holding in his arms a young goat. He sat himself down on a seat directly ahead of us and for a frightening moment he seemed to recognise Caroline, peering at her, smiling in an excited, half-mad way. She turned to the window, avoiding him, and at that point I saw that he was a Down's syndrome victim. I leaned towards Caroline and whispered in French. I was sure he would speak only Creole. At that, she relaxed slightly but kept her head turned away from him. It was then that I looked at the goat, its long, sinful face like a carnival devil's mask, its yellow, green-flecked orbs watching me, unblinking, the eyes of the evil one. I do not believe in the devil and not since boyhood have I feared hellfire. But, in some way I did not understand, it was as though the goat-eyes knew and incited my hidden desires. I heard my mother's dying voice:

Please, Paul. It is not too late. Leave the priesthood now.

The goat flicked its head upwards, its eyes closing in a shame-filled blink. I looked at Caroline Lambert, hiding in her nun's robe. She was seventeen years my junior, she was beautiful and foreign, someone from a world I could never enter. My longing for her was as unreal as that fleeting sight of the devil in the mask of a mindless goat.

There is only one hotel in Damienville, a dismal place where we ate in a dining room that smelled of rancid oil. Later, we were shown to rooms, small and squalid as cells. I tried to pray but could not. I lay on the dirty mattress, half-dozing, knowing that she lay a few doors away, my mind filled with the bitter irony of that beautiful, sensual face, framed in the purity of a religious robe.

Next morning I rented two mules and we set off up a twisting mountain track towards the region known as Pondicher. Here, in the high country, the air was thin and clear. Here, the land had not been endlessly divided among poor subsistence farmers, but belonged to a few rich families, people of Caroline's sort. As we climbed upwards, we could see below us clouds like great grey airships, drifting into the tops of tall pines. This was Ganae as it must have been centuries ago, in those unknown times of the Arunda Indians, before the French conquest, before black slaves, imported from Africa, won their freedom by butchering their owners in the years of revenge and revolt.

We were alone. No birds sang. All was silence. I was riding on muleback in a landscape magical as a painting by Poussin. I looked at her, riding ahead, her body bobbing in the saddle as the mule picked its way upwards, and again, I was suffused by a sense of loss for a path not taken, an unlived other life.

Shortly before noon we sat together on a rock, overlooking a steep canyon, eating sandwiches which I had purchased that morning in Damienville. She was telling me about her education at a convent of the Soeurs de Charité in Paris.

'I was twelve years old when I went to Paris. I had never been out of Ganae. I didn't know your world. I found out that the white people in France saw me as a *noir*. I cried a lot. How could they think I was black? Look at me. If you met me in the street in Paris would you think that I was a dirty black person?'

'Why is a black person dirty?'

'You haven't answered my question.'

'You haven't answered mine.'

She stared at me. 'Would you have done all this for me if I had been a black girl?'

'Yes. It has nothing to do with it.'

'Are you sure?'

I could not face her. I turned away.

'I'm sorry, Father. Forgive me. We were talking about the *noirs*. Even in Ganae, no one wants to be black.'

'That's not true.'

'No? Then why does every *noir* who comes to power try to send his children to your school? Why do his children try to become like us, to marry us, to live like us?'

'It isn't because of your colour,' I said. 'It's because you have everything and they have nothing. But, from now on, things are going to change. I know it.'

'Do you? Do you believe your friend Jeannot? He is a dirty black person, a little *noir arriviste*. He's jealous of us, he hates us. He wants to make this country into some sort of communist place. But nobody wants a communist place any more, do they? What's his policy? Tell me? He doesn't have one, does he? His policy is revenge, only revenge. And he's stupid. Ganae is not a big African country. It is a little island off Central America. And who cares about Central America? Ganae wasn't even a proper white man's colony. It is two hundred years since we drove the French out. The *noirs* here weren't trained by white colonists as they were in Africa and other places. All they're good for is labour, cheap labour. Our independence is a joke. We live on the edge of the white world, we depend on the white world. That will never change.'

I didn't answer her. I rose up and untied the mules. 'We must reach the convent before dark,' I said. 'Are you ready?'

Later that afternoon, she broke the silence that had descended on us. It was the moment when, in the distance, across the gulf of a ravine, we saw the stone buildings and tiled roofs of the convent. She reined in her mule and pointed. 'Is that where I will stay?'

'Yes.'

'When will you send for me?'

'Not for some weeks.'

'Are those nuns French?'

'Some of them. Reverend Mother is French.'

'So I am back in the convent with French nuns. Just like my schooldays. Who knows, perhaps I'll like being here. It will be a change. Maybe I'll become a nun.' She laughed and kicked her mule's sides. We moved on.

It was dark when I helped one of the convent servants unharness our weary animals. Reverend Mother had already taken Caroline Lambert up into the convent proper. As was usual with visiting priests, I was lodged in a small guest house near the stables. That night I dined alone in the convent parlour, waited on by an old nun who had been born in Boucherville, across the river from Montreal, and talked garrulously about her youth there in the time of Duplessis, a dictator of sorts, who once ruled that Canadian province.

In the morning, I said Mass for the nuns. As their attending priest came only on Sundays, this was an event. The church was full. The service was at seven. When I went up to the altar I looked to see if Caroline Lambert was present. She was not.

Later, after my breakfast in the convent parlour, I asked to see her.

'I believe she is still sleeping, Father,' Reverend Mother said. 'Shall I wake her?'

'No. It's not important. Tell her I will telephone her very soon.'

It rained that day as the mules picked their way back over twisted tracks and I came down through a mountain fog into the lower heights above Damienville. It was almost dark when I saw the tangled tin roofs of the town below me. As I came closer, night fell and soon, amid the flickering town lamps, a stronger light blazed. It was a bonfire on what seemed to be a rubbish dump just outside the first cluster of dwellings. A group of people, old and young, circled, singing. Jugs of *usque* were being passed around. It seemed to be a celebration of some sort. Then the dancing, drunken throng took up a new song. I listened, stiff with surprise. It was not a song but a hymn, Jeannot's favourite, 'Dieu et Patrie.'

I moved on past the bonfire. A few streets later, I entered the main square of Damienville. Here there was a second bonfire, but it was dying out. Some people were moving past it, silent, peering at the ebbing flames. As I came closer, my mule reared and made a hoarse honking sound. And then I saw that the back seat of a car had been placed on a heap of stones near the flames. Tied to the seat by two wires was a stout middle-aged man. He was dead, his body bloodied by what looked like sword cuts, his face bruised and blackened by blows. Someone had placed awkwardly on his head a blue-and-white seersucker forage cap of the type once worn by Doumergue's *bleus*.

Three old men were coming up the street, going towards the corpse. One of them, gap-toothed and foolish, looked over at me and called out, 'Justice, *Mon Pe*.'

'Who was he?'

'You don't know? Boulez, head of *bleus* here in time of

Uncle D. He want to push out Jeannot. Those *bleus* they trying to come back. Today we stop them. Justice time.'

He and the other men went up to the corpse. One of them leaned forward and awkwardly punched it in the stomach. 'Finish with you!' he yelled.

The other two turned and smiled at me, embarrassed, as though he had committed a social gaffe.

I watched them move off. The squalid hotel in which I had lodged the night before was just across the square. As I came up to it I saw a sign, scrawled on the wall with a charcoal stick.

BAS LES BLEUS

BAS LES BLANCS

MULÂTRES AU MUR

TOUCHE PAS NO' PE

When I reached the hotel I paid a bellboy to take the mules back to where I had rented them. I was too weary and sickened to eat the stringy chicken offered in the hotel dining room. As I handed back the menu and asked for some fruit, I heard a radio voice in the courtyard. I recognised the speaker: General Hemon, Army Chief of Staff.

'. . . in Mele. Four people were killed and several were injured including fifteen soldiers of the national guard. These figures, added to those I have already mentioned in the capital, make up a total of more than forty dead. To prevent further violence I have sent additional troops to each of the main centres and have instructed the commandant of the northern region to send reinforcements to Pondicher. President Cantave has expressed his sorrow for the deaths that have occurred. He will address parliament tomorrow morning at ten. In the meantime, the Army issues this warning. Demonstrators carrying machetes will be arrested. Looters will be shot.'

The national anthem started up when Hemon finished

speaking but after a few bars an announcer's voice said, 'We have received confirmation of our earlier report of property damage in the suburb of Bellevue. Shalimar, the mansion of Colonel Lambert where his wife, Caroline, entertained the international jet set, is reported to have been burned to the ground. In addition, demonstrators caused extensive damage to the residence of Senator Christian, leader of the Conservative Party, and ransacked the mansion of Herve Souter, the sporting goods millionaire, who is at present on holiday with his family on the Riviera. Troops of the Porte Riche Battalion have closed off all approaches to Bellevue. Only residents and official vehicles will be allowed access.'

I went out to the lobby and asked to use the telephone.

'I'm sorry, Father. Only emergency calls.'

'This is an emergency. I want to call the presidential palace.'

He smiled as if he did not believe me, then pushed the phone across the desk. 'Go ahead. Good luck.'

At first, I got a busy signal. Then an operator came on. 'All the lines to the palace have been closed until further notice. Please hang up.'

I looked at the concierge. 'I've been in the mountains,' I said. 'What's going on?'

'Nobody knows how it started. Rumours, I guess, but yesterday morning the radio said that the assembly has voted to throw Jeannot out. An hour later the assembly denied it, but it was too late. People were already in the streets. You saw the sign outside? TOUCHE PAS NO' PE. Leave our priest alone. Anyone who tries to get rid of Jeannot is asking for trouble.'

That night I had little sleep. At dawn I rose and went down the hall to the tin showers which were the only washing facility in the hotel. At that hour there was no service in the dining room and so I paid my bill and walked half-empty streets to the terminal where I boarded the first bus to Port Riche.

We travelled all day, stopping at every village on the route. My fellow travellers, most of them small traders, artisans, and servants of the rich, did not seem to know how the violence had begun. But one thing was certain. Everyone on the bus believed Jeannot's enemies were trying to get rid of him. 'They deny it, but we know it's true. Jeannot wants justice. They afraid of that. But it will happen. Caroline Lambert and the big capitalists like Herve Souter, all those bloodsuckers who hold us down. Justice time! It's over for them.'

When the bus finally pulled into the terminal that evening, I was unable to find a taxi. The streets of Port Riche were deserted. It was as though a curfew had been imposed and as I walked home in the half-dark streets I saw that even the beggars called *derniers*, solitary half-mad outcasts who camped in doorways, were huddled together for protection, a dozen of them sleeping in a semi-circle around the St Joseph fountain in the Rue Saint Sacrement with one of their number posted as a lookout on top of the saint's statue.

When I reached the residence, Hyppolite unlocked the main door which was double-bolted and chained.

'Want tea?'

'Yes, thank you.'

I went into the study. Noël Destouts was lying on the sofa, a book propped up on his huge stomach. 'Ah,' he said. 'So you're back already. How is Judge Letellier?'

I looked at him, surprised. I had forgotten my own lie.

'Better, thank God,' I said at last. 'But what's going on here?'

Noël heaved himself up into a sitting position. 'Constitutional crisis. There'll be a fight in parliament tomorrow. Our boy Jeannot against the rest. We should go and watch the fun.'

'How can we? What about classes?'

'It's Saturday,' he said. 'Don't you remember anything? Join me, why don't you? It should be interesting.'

Hyppolite arrived with cups of tea.

'All right. What time will it begin?'

'Around ten o'clock.'

Next morning we were late in starting because Noël over-slept. It was almost eleven when we reached the parliament buildings. After a security check we were admitted to the Spectators' Gallery overlooking the assembly. There are places never visited that, nevertheless, one feels one knows: stock exchanges, parliaments, courtrooms. But the sight of the Ganaen assembly in full session was unlike anything I could have imagined. Some of the congressmen and senators were armed, pistols strapped to their waists or holstered un-der their armpits. The Speaker made no attempt to preserve order. When we took our seats, Manes Planchon, the Mayor of Port Riche, a huge sweating *mulâtre*, wearing a Hawaiian shirt, cowboy boots and holstered revolver, was shouting at the top of his voice, 'You aren't the only one who was elected by the people, *Père* Cantave! This is a democracy, have you never heard of that word? We, too, were elected by the peo-ple! You think because you won big, that gives you all the power. Well, it doesn't. There are rules in this chamber. This is the assembly of the people, elected by the people. And you have been elected to obey these rules.'

I looked down at the front benches of the government where Jeannot sat. Some of those around him shouted back angrily but when he whispered to Pelardy his supporters' pro-test ceased. At this point, an elderly, elegant senatorial per-son, waving a large white silk handkerchief like a flag of truce, stepped down from the government benches, passing Jean-not, moving to the Speaker's podium.

'My party is the party of our President,' he cried. 'Or

should I say it *was* the party of our President. We who elected him have been shut out of the political process. Every recommendation we make is greeted with derision by a group of left-wing political amateurs who surround President Cantave. I ask you now, my President. Were these people appointed by you to be your *only* advisers? You have consistently ignored the party that chose you as its candidate. You have rejected the assembly's proposals for a qualified prime minister and are proposing a nobody who happens to be one of your toadies. At this point, with sadness in my heart, I must turn my back on you.'

From the opposition benches there were cheers and applause. The old man stood, as though undecided as to where he should now sit. At a nod from Pelardy, one of Jeannot's supporters rushed up to a microphone. 'Wait a minute, Senator. Do you think that the President of the United States or France would accept a prime minister picked by others? Ridiculous!'

Suddenly, someone among these lawmakers fired his revolver at the ceiling. The Speaker, roused at last, stood and shouted. 'That is dangerous! People could be killed. Sergeant, remove Congressman Laniel. Remove him at once!'

But nobody moved to remove the one who had fired the shot. Instead, two other shots were loosed off and the shouting became pandemonium. It was then that Jeannot rose up from the front bench, quiet and preoccupied as though he were alone in the room. He walked slowly towards the Speaker's chair. The shouting continued. He held up his hand, like a schoolboy asking to be recognised. Although the Speaker did not acknowledge his gesture, the din died down.

Jeannot stood waiting, looking up at the ceiling of the chamber, until there was near silence. Then, in that extraordinary transformation that came over him when he faced an audience, he began.

Brothers,
Friends and Enemies,
And yes, my enemies who are my friends,
I speak to you, to all of you today.
My Brothers,
We who have been elected to serve our country,
All of us, yes, all of us, were elected to this chamber.
I do not deny that. Why should I deny it?
The people have chosen us, yes,
But remember that God speaks through the people
And so God has chosen us,
All of us,
Even those who carry guns and swear untruths.
Even those who toady to the rich and rob the poor.
God has placed you in this chamber.
I do not ask you to elect Hercule Harsant as prime
    minister
Because I want to rule through him.
I ask you because
God has placed me here to serve the poor.
Because
I have prayed to Jesus who is my Lord and master,
I have asked Him to put into this mouth of mine
Words which will make you know,
All of you—even you, my friend and enemy,
Manes Planchon. And you, Longvy, and you, Parigot.
All of you,
That my cause is just.
That my path is the true path.
And you must also know
That I am no one.
That I have no ambitions.
And yet
I speak for Jesus.
Jesus is the poor.

I speak for them.
Some of you are angry because Ganae is changing.
Because the people
Will no longer stand still.
They will no longer stand for parliamentary rules
Or parliamentary tricks.
Already, it has begun.
The time of the machete.
What do I mean by that?
I mean the trouble we have seen these past days.
Mansions of the rich have been burned down.
People have been killed.
These things have happened and we sorrow for the dead.
But we do not repent.
Vengeance is mine, saith the Lord.
Justice must be done.
It has not yet been done.
We cannot start to feed our people,
We cannot start to give them a decent, humble life.
If we are not united,
If we are not strong,
The poor cannot be free.
Unless they are rid of those who exploit them.
You know who I am talking about,
I do not have to spell it out again.
But what I have to say now, I have not said before.
Justice is a sword.
It has been put into the hands of my people.
My people are the poor.
The sword of the poor is used to cut down cane.
It is a humble sword.
Machete.
A rough tool, made of iron.
I say to you now.
The humble sword awaits us.

It will punish us.
It is tired of our brawling,
It is tired of this chamber.
It cannot wait much longer.
I warn you, my Brothers.
Beware that sword.
Machete.
If it is raised against you
It will be because you failed the poor.
Put away your revolvers.
They will not help you.
You have soldiers and tanks
But none of it will help you
Against the sword.
Do as the people ask.
Let us have justice.
I speak for them. I act for them.
I am nothing.
But I am God's servant.
God has given me this sword.
I warn you.
Do as the people ask.
And do it now.

The chamber was silent as a church. I stared down at the heads of the lawmakers as they watched this slight, boyish figure turn from the Speaker's podium and make his way down the chamber. No one moved to stop him or to follow him. The flunkies guarding the doors threw them open. Jeannot walked out. At once, the silence ended in pandemonium. Manes Planchon drew his revolver and fired it, bringing a momentary pause in which he shouted, 'You heard? You heard? Who is the violent one? *He* is!'

Noël and I were already on our feet. We hurried towards the exit and down the stairs to the ground floor. When we ran outside we saw, driving through the main gateway, a black Mercedes flying the presidential colours.

'I'm going to the palace,' I said. 'Will I drop you off?'

He nodded. 'What will you do there?'

'I must talk to him.'

'Too late. Remember Diderot. "Between fanaticism and barbarism there's only one step." Jeannot's just taken that step.'

'You don't understand.'

'No, I don't,' Noël said. 'Do you?'

NINE

I DROPPED NOËL OFF at the residence and drove directly to the palace. There was no sign of anything unusual in the great square surrounding it but when I passed through the gates I saw a phalanx of Jeannot's picked 'soldiers' stationed at all approaches to the presidential offices. I was recognised by one of his aides, who told me he was not in the building but had left for Radio Libre a few minutes ago.

'What time is the broadcast?'

The aide said no one knew.

I left the palace and drove through the market area hoping to catch up with Jeannot at the radio station. As I did, I saw an unusually large number of people in the streets. On Avenue Domville a traffic jam evolved and slowed my passage to a crawl. I had no radio in my car. While I sat stalled in traffic Jeannot was broadcasting to the nation. And so I did not hear the most fateful speech of his career. It was the 'machete' speech, a version of what he had already said in parliament that morning. But now he spoke to the possessors of that 'humble sword,' telling them that, with it, they, the people, could rule. The elite and the politicians wanted to install a prime minister who was their creature. The people must say no.

I never did get to speak to Jeannot that day. He had left the radio station by the time I reached it. Within an hour of his speech, Port Riche became a city in crisis. The voices heard on the radio and blaring from army trucks were the voices of General Hemon and his aides appealing for calm, threatening looters, denying reports of violence. But there was violence. That afternoon Father Duchamp saw the bodies of four people shot by soldiers in the mud-clotted lanes of La Rotonde. Six dead rioters were brought to the morgue of Charité Hospital and the nuns there treated some thirty wounded. Four soldiers were hacked to pieces when they tried to stop a mob which broke into the parliament yard and overturned official limousines.

Violence was not confined to the capital. The radio station in Papanos said that Senator Lutyens, his wife and two sons, had been butchered by machetes and their bodies placed on a burning pyre in the city's main square. Senator Lutyens was a former ambassador to Washington, a Doumerguist and Papanos's leading businessman.

After supper that night I passed by Father Bourque's study. The door was open and he called out to me.

'Is that you, Paul?'

He was sitting in his old rattan armchair facing a window that looked out on the nearby roofs of La Rotonde. The window was open and in the distance we heard the sound of shouts and chanting. Clouds of smoke from bonfires rose above the tin roofs of the slums. 'The Archbishop just called me,' Father Bourque said. 'As you know, he and I haven't been friends over the years so he's the last person in the world to ask for my help. But he did. He wanted to know if I could do anything to stop Jeannot. Or if you could. I said I'd speak to you but I didn't have much hope.'

'Both sides are doing the killing,' I said.

'That's not the point. You heard about Senator Lutyens and his family. It's terrible. Terrible. Has Jeannot no conscience at all?'

'Jeannot didn't order these things. I imagine he's as distressed as we are.'

'Is he? I wonder. Machetes! Machetes! I'm sick when I think of it.'

As he was speaking, the telephone rang. It was an enquiry from a parent. Would the college be open tomorrow? There were reports of attacks on *mulâtre* children. I listened as Father Bourque tried to reassure the caller. When he put down the phone he asked me, 'Have you heard anything about these attacks?'

I said, and it was true, that the city was filled with rumours, most of them false. I said if I could be excused from classes in the morning I would go to the palace and try to find out what was going on.

'I'd be grateful if you would,' Father Bourque said. 'And Paul? If you still have any influence with Jeannot, now is the time to use it.'

My room, the same room I have today, is on the side of the residence facing La Rotonde. At night because of the heat I keep the windows open. I have long been accustomed to night noises and normally I sleep soundly. But that night I was wakened shortly after two A.M. by police sirens and gunfire. When I got up and looked out of my window, I saw a gang of about twenty youths coming from La Rotonde into Rue Pelikan. They were carrying machetes and running at full tilt. The sirens grew louder and two riot trucks loaded with armed police careened into sight in pursuit of the youths, who split up, running in differing directions. The police trucks stalled, sirens wailing to a standstill as the officer in charge searched for the best route to continue the pursuit.

After some minutes the police drove off, their chase abandoned.

Next morning I was due to say the eight o'clock Mass at the college. At seven-fifteen, while I was shaving, Hyppolite knocked and said, '*Pe* Destouts on telephone, wants you now.'

Noël Destouts was due to say the seven o'clock Mass. Perhaps he had been taken ill? When I picked up the phone Noël spoke in a low voice as though he might be overheard. 'Paul, can you come over to the chapel at once? I'm just going to start Mass. Wait for me in the sacristy. It's urgent.'

Noël was the last person in the world to be alarmist. Normally, I walk to the chapel but that morning I took the school car, our little white Peugeot. The streets seemed quiet. A light rain was falling. The school chapel sits across the road from the college. When I went into the chapel I saw that only about a dozen people were attending the service. Noël, who always said Mass quickly, was already coming up to the last gospel, so I went into the sacristy, knowing I would only have a few minutes to wait.

There was no one in the sacristy. No one living, that is. Under the bench that was used to lay out vestments I saw a large purple dustcloth of the sort that covers church statues in Holy Week. It was draped over a body. The heels of polished boots protruded from one end. Part of the cloth was stained, its purple colour darkened by what looked like blood. Outside, in the chapel, I heard coughing and movement of benches as the congregation began to leave. I went over and lifted the cloth. Priests see death more often than do other men. But now my hand trembled as it held the cloth. The face was hacked by knife cuts, the body an oozing mess. Machetes had slashed again and again at the torso and head, ripping the fabric of the military uniform so that dead flesh bulged out. The eyes were open and stared past me as though in the moment of his death Colonel Maurras had seen something he would be for ever condemned to watch. I pulled the cover back over the body. Sitting on a ledge by the window was his wallet, folded back to show a military pass and a photograph which bore his name.

Behind me, the sacristy door opened and Noël said to his altar boy, 'Take your surplice over to the school. I have to speak to Father Paul. You can bring it here later.'

'Yes, Father.'

Noël came in, shutting the door behind him. He put down chalice and paten and began to untie his chasuble. 'Have you looked at it?'

'Yes.'

'Maurras,' he said. 'He was the one you told me would come here with a political message. Right?'

'Yes. What happened?'

'The night porter found the body outside the school gates about five o'clock this morning. Someone rang the bell and when he went down to investigate he saw half a dozen young men walking away from the gates. They carried machetes. He didn't unlock the gate but left the body where it lay in the street. He was afraid to touch it. This morning, when I came to say Mass, he was waiting for me. I searched the body, found that wallet and knew it was the man you were expecting. So I helped the porter carry the body in here. Who was Maurras?'

'Do you remember the boy we buried a few years ago? Shot by a colonel of the president's guard?'

'I'd forgotten,' Noël said. 'But obviously some people have not. Were they Jeannot's boys, do you think?'

I didn't answer. I said I would have to tell Jeannot at once. 'Leave the body here. Don't let anyone in. Tell them the eight o'clock Mass has been cancelled.'

Noël looked at the shrouded corpse. 'Do you think he was on his way here to tell you something?'

'That's what I have to find out.'

The streets were still quiet. The great square surrounding

the palace was empty of army vehicles. I parked my car in the usual place and walked towards the ornamental gates. Jeannot's 'soldiers' were still on guard there. I began to take heart. I was admitted and led to Pelardy's office. Jeannot was there, talking on the telephone. I went up to him. At once, he covered the mouthpiece with his hand. 'What is it, Paul?'

'The Colonel.'

He put the phone down at once and turned to Pelardy and Mathieu Clément. 'I have to speak to Paul. If you'll just wait outside? It's something private.'

When they left the room I told him what had happened. He listened, then asked, 'Was he on his way to warn us?'

'You mean who killed him? Your people or theirs?'

'*Theirs?*'

'It could be that they killed him and left him at the college gates to warn you that you're no longer safe.'

'Why would they do that?'

'Because, if you're afraid of a coup, you'll send people back into the streets to show your strength. Which may be just what the plotters want.'

He stared at me. 'What do you mean?'

'Jeannot, if this violence continues, they won't need to stage a coup. The outside world will turn against your regime. And as soon as that happens, don't count on your friend General Hemon. The Army will take over the government for the sake of "restoring public order." It's a trap as old as the history of Ganae. And I think you're falling into it.'

'You're wrong,' he said. 'This is a revolution and it's just beginning.'

'Is it? What sort of revolution? The Army and the elite have the guns. If it comes to an open conflict thousands of our people will be killed. Even if this thing hadn't happened with Maurras, I was going to speak to you today. I was going to tell you that you're responsible for these deaths. It's hard for me to say this, I who respect you, who look up to you, who think of you as a sort of saint.'

'Oh Paul,' he said. 'I'm no saint. But, don't you know how much I hate this killing?'

'Then end it,' I said. 'It's terrible and it's working against you.'

'But do I have the right to end it? What will happen if our people give up the struggle? What does God want me to do?'

Suddenly, Pelardy hurried into the room. 'Jeannot, there are some army vehicles moving into the square outside. I don't know. Is something wrong?'

Jeannot turned to me. 'If *they* killed Maurras, that means they know he's told us their plans. And it could mean they're about to move against me. Do you have your car here?'

'It's parked in the public car-park across the square.'

He went to the door and opened it. 'Mathieu?'

Mathieu Clément came in at once.

'Mathieu, make out a special pass for Father Paul's car to come in at the rear entrance to the palace. We're going to drive, incognito, to Radio Libre where I'll go on the air and make a special announcement. No one must see us leave. Once I've finished at the radio station we'll drive to Lavallie. We mustn't be followed.'

'What's going on? Why Lavallie?' Pelardy asked.

'Pele, my life may be in danger. We've got to get out of here. Mathieu, hurry! Get Paul's pass.'

Ten minutes later I was sitting in my little white Peugeot outside the palace kitchens where several provisions vans were unloading the day's food. When Jeannot came out of the building with Pelardy and Mathieu Clément, he was wearing a white cotton shirt and trousers, his head completely covered by a large floppy straw hat of the type that sugar-cane cutters used in the fields. None of the servants or delivery men noticed him. As we drove back up to the rear entrance, again, I waved my special pass at the soldiers on duty. They barely glanced at it. We drove out in silence and at once, in the great square, I saw that things had changed. The immense space, empty minutes ago, was crowded with army vehicles. There were even three tanks lined up in front of the main gates. In the courtyard, soldiers stood in riot formation, facing the presidential quarters. There was no sign of Jeannot's personal guards. Two army staff cars were parked at the main doorway. One flew a general's flag.

We drove out of the square. On the Avenue de la République shopkeepers were hastily pulling down iron shutters over windows and doors. Others were loading goods into taxis as though preparing to flee the city. On every street corner soldiers stood, holding automatic rifles, laughing and joking as though they had been summoned to a fête. Further up the street we heard shots. We passed a group of children who were hurling rocks at the already shattered windscreens of two cars. In the Rue Desmoulins some market stalls had been looted and wrecked. Spoiled fruit was scattered across the road.

'I think we were lucky,' Jeannot said. 'If we'd waited ten more minutes we'd have been too late.'

'If that's so,' I said, 'they'll have control of the radio stations.'

'Let's find out,' Jeannot said.

Radio Libre is a two-storey concrete building on a hill overlooking the Meredieu district. In the days of the dictator it was surrounded by a barbed-wire fence, its gates controlled by electricity and manned by Doumergue's *bleus*. After Doumergue's death the gates were left open and the guards removed. And now as we drove up, the gates were open. There were no soldiers about. Everything seemed normal. But suddenly Jeannot said, 'Turn round, Paul. Don't go in.'

'What is it?'

'Look.' He pointed to the entrance. An old beige Cadillac

was parked there. Beside it, a police car and a police motor cycle. 'That's Raymond's car,' Jeannot said. 'Remember what Maurras told you. "Raymond will be at the radio station ready to broadcast as soon as he hears they've taken over the palace." '

I turned the car round. 'Take a left up ahead,' Jeannot said. 'That's Avenue Mouton. There's a café on the corner called L'Américaine. I spoke there during the elections. They have radio and a television set. If the coup has been announced they'll know about it.'

When we drove up to the place he had indicated he said, 'Mathieu, you go in. We'll stay in the car.'

Mathieu did as he was bid. It was a big café, open early because it was near the cattle market and served breakfasts of steak and Cuban beer. I parked the car half a block away. The café was crowded, not with customers but with people who had come in off the street to find out the news. Mathieu went inside. We watched him talk to some men who were sitting near the television set.

At that point, about thirty people came out of the cattle market holding up two large placards with Jeannot's picture. They passed by us, singing the hymn 'Dieu et Patrie.'

'Those people know,' Jeannot said. 'We have our answer.'

As if to confirm it, Mathieu came out of the café and hurried towards the car. When Mathieu got in, Jeannot touched me on the shoulder. 'Drive on. We're going to Lavallie.'

'Raymond made a speech on radio about fifteen minutes ago,' Mathieu said. 'According to him, you've been removed by parliament because of your refusal to govern by democratic means. The general assembly has appointed Raymond premier until elections can be held. He also said you're believed to have fled the country.'

'They're pretending it isn't a military coup,' Jeannot said. 'But as long as I'm free and able to contact a radio station, that lie isn't going to work.'

We were coming on to the road that leads from Port Riche into the mountains where Lavallie is situated. It was a main road, one of six that led out of the city. Ahead, amid the trudging lines of peasants bringing their bundles to market, was the usual hodge-podge of old cars, camionettes and mule carts moving in and out of the capital. But, as we came closer, we crawled along so slowly that we were moving little faster than the pedestrians marching along the sides of the road.

'Roadblock,' Pelardy said.

Straddling the road were two army trucks and an armoured car, a machine gun swivelling on its turret. The officer in charge of the operation was a *mulâtre* with the rank of captain.

Jeannot, when he saw the officer, turned to Pelardy. 'Why is it a captain? Because they need someone who'll recognise me, someone who'll be able to control the soldiers who might let me through.'

'It will be the same at all other exit roads from the city,' Pelardy said. 'And they'll have a watch on the airport and the docks.'

'If we could get past this lot,' Mathieu Clément said, 'there's a coastal village outside Lavallie. We might be able to rent a fishing boat to take us to Cuba.'

'I can't leave,' Jeannot said. 'People must know that I'm here, that I haven't been killed.'

'What will we do, then?'

'We must try to get to Callil. Father Pat Redmond—remember his radio station? It's local, so they've probably overlooked it.'

We were still about two hundred yards from the roadblock. 'All right,' Jeannot said. 'The rest of you go through. They don't know you.'

He motioned me to stop the car. He got out and slipped into the queue of men and women who were trudging along the edge of the road. I saw him speak to a woman who was laden with baskets. He took some of the baskets and fell in behind her. In his cane cutter's floppy hat, his worn shirt and trousers, he looked no different from the others. The soldiers ahead, intent on checking the vehicles on the road, were paying little attention to the pedestrians who shuffled past the armoured car.

Our line of vehicles speeded up. We left Jeannot behind. When we reached the roadblock, the officer looked first at me, the *blanc*, and then at Pelardy, the *mulâtre*.

'Where are you going?'

'To the St Viateur School,' I said.

He nodded and waved us on.

We drove slowly and pulled in at a turn in the road, out of sight of the soldiers. When I saw Jeannot coming towards us, still part of the peasant group, I thanked God for his deliverance. But when Jeannot got into the car and we drove slowly on in the stream of rickety vehicles my prayer mocked me. What deliverance?

Then, confirming my fears, Pelardy said to Jeannot, 'I've been thinking. You shouldn't risk a radio address. It's far too dangerous. You should try for asylum in one of the embassies and put your case from there. It's not going to be easy for you. Raymond's saying this is a political upset. Unfortunately, the world's going to believe him.'

'Nonsense,' Jeannot said.

'Is it? Your "machete" speech was reported in all the foreign media. Since then we've had street riots, property burned down, people killed. That's what the world is hearing about. And there'll be more of it once our people realise that they've lost their little priest.'

'They haven't lost me,' Jeannot said. 'When I go on radio they'll rise up and turn these plotters out. And the world will back *us*. We represent democracy, we were freely elected. The United Nations—every parliament, every country—will be on our side.'

'If you go on radio,' Pelardy said, 'the Army will make sure you don't do it twice. This is a small island. They'll find you and kill you.'

Jeannot turned around and smiled at Pelardy who was sitting in the back seat. 'I know you don't believe in God, Pele. But God is here, He is with us now and He, not I, dictates these events. If it's His will that I be killed, then I must accept it. In the meantime, we'll go to Callil.'

We drove on. Two miles up the road, I turned off on a small road that led to the Pondicher region. For the next twenty miles, the only vehicles we saw were three heavy old army trucks laden with vegetables, which passed us slowly, going in the opposite direction. A sergeant sitting on top of the load was listening to a blaring portable radio. The announcer was speaking in Creole. I couldn't catch the words.

'Did you hear?' Jeannot asked. 'He said something about a riot in Mele. That means they haven't taken over the radio stations yet. If they had, they'd never let that news get out.'

I looked at him. He was smiling and cheerful as I'd rarely seen him in these last weeks. He saw my look and said, 'Cheer up, Paul. We're winning. I know it.'

Shortly after two o'clock we reached Callil, a large village which had grown up around two coffee plantations owned by a wealthy mulatto family who lived in Port Riche. The peasants who worked in these plantations lived in huts made of wooden frames, walled with mud-daubed wattles and thatched with palm branches and guinea grass. Approaching Callil, one could imagine oneself in rural Africa. But in the past ten years, with help from Jeannot and his boys' club workers, Father Pat Redmond of the Holy Ghost Fathers had built a church, an elementary school and, because he was a fervent radio ham, a small transmitting station from which he broadcast sermons and news of the region. Redmond, a carrot-haired Irish priest, was a natural rebel, often in trouble with his religious superiors. He was one of Jeannot's strongest supporters.

Now his parishioners, seeing our car, ran down to the village well, where Redmond was at work repairing the pump. 'Jeannot! Jeannot, *ici*!'

At once it seemed that half the occupants of the village came running out of their dwellings and up from the coffee groves to cluster around Jeannot, cheering, embracing him as he got out of the car. 'Wait, wait,' I heard him say. 'Were soldiers here today?'

'Not today. They came two days ago. We had a demonstration but they stopped it. They took Marie-Claire Boulez and her husband. Shot them. There.' They pointed to a crucifix of palm branches and a wreath of frangipani placed against a wall of the village school.

At that moment I saw Pat Redmond come up the rutted path from the well, red-faced, and a little out of breath, his cassock hiked up around his waist showing baggy khaki trousers and heavy workboots. Attached to his belt was a small radio which he shut off as he came towards us. Jeannot went to him, asking, 'You heard about the coup?'

'Of course.' He pointed to the radio on his belt. 'I've been listening all morning.'

'Tell us,' Pelardy said. 'We have no radio.'

'Macandal's plane arrived from Paris an hour ago. Lambert is with him. General Hemon has stepped down as Army Chief of Staff. So it looks as if you've lost your backing.'

'The people will back me,' Jeannot said.

Redmond hesitated, then said, 'Jeannot, you're not safe here. The Margitals have their spies. They're probably phoning them from the plantation office, right this minute.'

The Margitals were the plantation owners. I had thought of the same thing. But Jeannot said, 'We won't stay long. I came to make a broadcast. Is that possible? I've got to let people know that I'm safe.'

Redmond glanced at the expectant villagers clustered around us. 'Let's go inside.'

He led us into the schoolhouse where children sat at home-made desks, listening to Father Rourke, a Holy Ghost Father in his twenties, who had recently come to help run the parish. We went into Pat's crowded office, one part of which was partitioned off and filled with his radio equipment.

But he did not take us in there. Instead, he shut the outer door of the office and said, 'We've had a lot of trouble here. The day after your "machete" speech our people marched down to the plantation office asking for proper wages. The Margitals were scared and called in the soldiers. Two people were shot to death and I had to send fourteen others, some of them kids, over to the hospital in Melun. It was like the old days with Doumergue's *bleus*. Brutal.'

'I'm sorry,' Jeannot said.

'Are you?'

We were standing in a semi-circle, Pelardy, Mathieu Clément, myself, Pat, Jeannot. In the other room we heard children's voices recite a verse. Behind the desk an old wall clock ticked away. I stared at Pat's sun-reddened Irish face, his cold, blue, Gaelic eyes.

Then Jeannot said, 'Of course I'm sorry that these things happened. But I'm not ashamed of it. The people themselves will make the revolution. I am only the catalyst. This morning, the elite tried to get rid of me. They failed. I am here. I am still President. When people find that out they will go into the streets again and demand that I be reinstated. I'm not asking for violence. I ask for justice. Democracy must prevail.'

'And if it doesn't,' Pat Redmond said, 'how many of our people will be killed? Half an hour ago I spoke with friends over the short-wave radio. The streets of Port Riche, Mele, Doumergueville and Papanos are filled with soldiers. Maybe, the only thing that really works in this country is the staging of a coup. They've taken over Radio Libre—'

'I know that,' Jeannot said. 'That's why I'm here. I don't know anything about radio but if I speak on your transmitter it will be picked up, won't it? Abroad, as well?'

'It's not only your speech that will be picked up,' Pat said. 'You'll be picked up. Once they find out where the broadcast is coming from, they'll close off all roads to Callil in half an hour. Where will you hide?'

'People will hide me,' Jeannot said. 'But that's not important. The important thing is that I speak out now. That the truth is broadcast to the rest of the world, to the United Nations, to the Organisation of American States. If that happens they'll never get away with this. Will you help me?'

'No.'

We stood there, all of us, as though shot by that one word. We were the faithful and Jeannot was our leader. He had helped Pat build his church and build the schoolhouse we stood in. He was asking for something vital, something only Pat could give.

'Are you afraid?' Jeannot said.

'Yes. This is my parish, these are my people. If we help you, we'll be punished. They won't shoot me, but they will shoot men, women and kids who can't read or write, who never heard of the United Nations or the OAS, who marched down to the Margitals' office last week because you told them to. You say you won't preach violence but it's too late for that. Violence has begun. The people believe in you. They will march against armed soldiers to defend you. They think of you as the Messiah. I don't.'

'If only I were,' Jeannot said. He went up to Pat and embraced him. 'All right, Pat. Follow your conscience. That's what they taught us.'

He turned to Mathieu Clément. 'There's another possibility, do you remember that station in Cap Gauche, the one run by Willi—Willi something?'

'Willi Narodny,' Mathieu said. 'He's a wild man.'

'And he doesn't have a parish,' Jeannot said. He turned back to Pat. 'Can I use your phone? Is that all right?'

'I can do better than that,' Pat said. 'Willi's a ham. We talk all the time. Come in here.'

He led Jeannot into the room that was his radio station. As they went in, Jeannot closed the door, leaving me, Mathieu and Pelardy alone in the outer office.

'He should go to an embassy,' Pelardy said. 'Tell him, Father. He'll listen to you.'

'He won't.'

'How far is Cap Gauche from here?' Pelardy asked Mathieu.

'An hour. But we have to go through Papanos. Pat said it's full of soldiers, remember?'

'I'm not going with you,' Pelardy said.

We looked at him.

'Because you're not going to make it. Let me go back to Port Riche. I'll go to the Canadian Embassy and ask for their help. If we could get him in there, he'd be safe.'

But when, a few minutes later, Jeannot and Pat came out of the radio room and Pelardy made his suggestion, Jeannot said at once, 'A prisoner in an embassy, surrounded by Lambert's soldiers, waiting for the big world to help me out? No thanks.' He turned to me. 'Paul, will you take me to Cap Gauche? I've spoken to Willi. His station hasn't been shut down. He's been told he can stay on the air but he must issue no news bulletins until he's given one by the coup leaders. He's obeyed so far, but he's willing to help me.'

Pelardy said, 'Jeannot, let me tell you one thing. You don't understand politics, you never will. If you want to be a martyr, I can't stop you. But if you go on to Papanos and are arrested, it will be the end of everything we fought for. I'm going back to Port Riche.'

Jeannot turned to Mathieu. 'And you?'

'I'm your press secretary,' Mathieu said. 'You want to make a broadcast. Fine.'

And so we stood there with Jeannot in that room, two who would go with him, two who had refused him. Jeannot made no difference between us. As he had embraced Pat Redmond, he now embraced Pelardy.

'Pele, I want to thank you for all you've done. In a few weeks this will be behind us. You'll be back in your old office telling me what to do.'

We went outside. A crowd of some fifty people waited, as though they expected Jeannot to make a speech. Instead, he waved to them and walked quickly to the car. People, seeing him leave, ran to him, crowding around him, touching him as though he were some sort of talisman. When we reached the car, Pat Redmond called out, 'Jeannot, just a minute.' He then unhooked the little portable radio from his belt. 'Take this. At least you'll know what's going on.'

Then Redmond, who was a foot taller than Jeannot, bent down and scooped him into his arms as though he were a child. 'God bless you, lad. Safe journey.'

And so we set off. I drove. Mathieu sat beside me while Jeannot, in the back seat, endlessly spun the radio dial. The stations of Ganae played mindless Java music. At last he caught a Spanish-language voice broadcasting from San Juan. Jeannot spoke Spanish. He listened, becoming more and more excited at what he heard. 'Do you know what's happened? Everyone—the American government, the OAS, the French—everyone refuses to recognise Raymond as premier! Americans say they will cut off aid.'

The Spanish-language station was now broadcasting other news. Jeannot again fiddled with dials. We heard a voice from Barbados. 'The Port Riche International Airport has been closed and a Reuter's correspondent was attacked by soldiers as he attempted to enter an area of the slums where the Army is shooting at rioters. The rioters are supporters of Father

Cantave, the deposed president. Canada and France have responded to the OAS appeal and have withdrawn assistance programmes to Ganae totalling some forty-eight million dollars.'

'You see,' Jeannot said excitedly, 'they won't get away with it.'

'Jeannot,' Mathieu Clément said. 'Listen to me. Pele was right. I think you should try to find asylum in one of the embassies. The world is on your side now. Let the OAS do your fighting for you.'

'I will, after the broadcast,' Jeannot said. 'But first, people must hear my voice.'

Jeannot was listening again to a Spanish-language broadcast as I drove our little Peugeot off the gravelly side road and on to a pot-holed main highway which led towards Papanos. Soon, we overtook a local bus and passed it. But the road was curiously empty. No market women walked its rim bearing their daily burdens, no donkeys laden with charcoal impeded our passage. We stared ahead waiting for a sight of army vehicles. But even as we came within a few miles of Papanos, the road was deserted.

Now, on the horizon, we saw a heavy column of smoke.

'What is it, a bonfire?' Jeannot asked.

'It's bigger than that,' Mathieu said.

At a turn in the road people came towards us on foot, carrying bundles and babies, a very old woman being pulled along in a makeshift cart, a man herding three goats. They were peasants. When they saw our car approaching they hesitated, as though afraid of us.

I stopped the car. Mathieu got out and went towards the people. After a few minutes, Mathieu came back and got in.

'Soldiers have burned their village. They say people were shot and thrown in a ditch.'

'But why?' Jeannot said.

'When the radio announced the coup, the village people

came out of their houses calling for you. After a while army units drove in from Papanos. The villagers threw rocks at them. The soldiers opened fire, then burned the village down. They say the Army's still there.'

'Should we go on?' Mathieu asked.

'We must.'

I drove on. When we came to the village I saw that the huts had been reduced to smoking, skeletal frames. A few people sat in the middle of the ruins. We drove past them slowly. They did not look up. At the far end of the village three army trucks were zig-zagged across the road. From one of them we heard the static of an intercom. The soldiers, about twenty of them, were sitting on the ground, eating their midday meal. For a moment I thought they would ignore us, but as we drove up to them, a sergeant put down his plate, got up and pointed a rifle at me. I stopped. He slung the rifle over his shoulder and came towards us, unhooking a clipboard from his belt. I rolled down the window. He looked in, then handed me the clipboard and a pencil.

'Put down your licence number. Where are you going? Papanos?'

'Further. St Viateur.'

I wrote down the number on the line he indicated. The licence numbers of other vehicles were listed above mine, written in different hands. He looked at what I had put down, walked to the front of the car to check it against the licence plate, then waved us on. As we drove up the road, Jeannot said, 'He's calling in our number.'

Through the rear-view mirror I saw that the Sergeant was using the truck's intercom. 'Licensed to the Collège St Jean,' Mathieu said. 'Right?'

'Yes.'

'Driven by a *blanc* priest. They'll know it's you, Father.'

'We got through,' Jeannot said. 'God is telling us: "Keep going." '

Ten minutes later we reached Papanos. At first the city seemed deserted, shops shuttered, streets empty of traffic. But as we drove closer to the centre we came upon overturned vehicles, shopfronts broken into, and, a strange sight, some fifteen pigs moving across a square, rooting in and eating from heaps of rubbish. Suddenly, there were soldiers everywhere, some in army trucks, some in a variety of vehicles which they had commandeered, camionettes, taxi-buses, private cars, delivery vans. They drove aimlessly through the streets at the city's centre, blowing horns, firing off rifles at random. Sometimes, soldiers leaped down from a vehicle, to smash a shop window and loot its contents, sometimes they poked open guns from car windows and took potshots at chimneys, stray cats, billboards and lampposts. Because of this, the streets were empty and the few people who had been caught unawares huddled in doorways, trying to keep out of sight. Once, a soldier poked a gun at us and, grinning, fired over our heads. It was a scene of macabre carnival, fragmented as in a disturbed and senseless dream.

Jeannot turned on the radio and we heard a voice speaking in Creole. 'We ask for understanding, we ask the people of Ganae to show, once again, their great patriotic virtues—'

'That's Raymond,' Mathieu said.

'We ask that you, our honest citizens, abstain from demonstrations and public meetings during this state of emergency. We ask that each town and village of the nation observe the curfew which will go into effect this evening from eight P.M. until eight A.M. The Army warns that those who do not obey the curfew risk being shot as looters. We ask for healing—we ask for—'

But I no longer heard the radio. I was deafened by a chorus of car horns demanding that I get out of the way. I pulled into the side of the road to let six army trucks rush by. Soldiers stood up in these trucks, drinking jugs of *usque* and shouting the lyrics of an obscene song. When they were out of sight, we drove on to the edge of town, taking the fork that led to Cap Gauche. As we left Papanos we saw, in a ditch at the crossroads, two dead men, a dead pregnant woman and two small, frightened children. The adults had been shot in the head, execution style. As we passed by, the children, seeing us, cowered down in the ditch, hiding behind the bodies, their hands covering their heads as though to ward off invisible blows.

I turned to look at Jeannot. He sat at the window staring down at the children. The excitement I had seen in his face when he listened to the Spanish radio was replaced by a look of desolation. What must he be thinking, he who was at the centre of these events?

As we drove on, Mathieu Clément said, 'Those soldiers are like wild animals! My God! Why do they let them loose like this?'

'It's part of a plan,' Jeannot said. 'The soldiers are poor, they're *noir*, they might turn against their masters and join the people. So the Army encourages them to get drunk and loot and fire off guns. When that happens, people hide from uniforms. The Army becomes lawless. And, all at once, it's the only law in the land.'

I looked at him. His voice was calm as though he were explaining a lesson to a student. But he was weeping. He wiped the back of his hand over his eyes. 'How far to Cap Gauche?' he asked.

'Another half-hour,' Mathieu said.

I looked at the road ahead. I heard the radio crackling. Now, on the band, the only sound was music, coming from Radio Libre, Radio Mele and Radio Nord. Here, as we climbed into the mountains, the foreign stations were lost in static. Jeannot switched off.

'Look out!' Mathieu said suddenly. Ahead, coming around a bend in the road, were two army trucks. Soldiers stood up in them, singing. The trucks came rushing down the crown of the road as though our car were invisible. I swerved to the right, skidded, corrected the skid and, at that moment, the first truck passed by me. The singing soldiers were drunk. Someone fired off a rifle. The second truck was on me now and it was as though the driver wanted to force us off the road. Again I swerved, our old car running dangerously close to the ragged shoulder and the deep ditch below it. I was trying to keep the car on the road and, at first, did not hear the second round of shots. Part of my windshield shattered, coruscating into a maze of patterns. On the right-hand side of the car where Mathieu sat, I heard the ping of bullets as they struck the door.

'Keep going!' Jeannot shouted.

The soldiers in the second truck had also been taking potshots at our car but now, when I looked back, both trucks were disappearing down the roadway. At that moment Mathieu, sitting beside me, slumped forward, his forehead striking the shattered windshield. Blood trickled from his ear. I braked. Jeannot jumped out and came around to Mathieu's door. He had trouble opening it because the bullets had forced it out of shape. Jeannot reached in and, staggering, lifted Mathieu out of the car and put him down by the side of the road. He took Mathieu's bloodied face in his hands and I saw his lips move in prayer.

I did not know Mathieu as he did. I knew that Mathieu was twenty-nine years old, the son of a *neg riche*, a successful *noir* rice trader. He had studied at our college and won an American scholarship which took him to the Columbia School of Journalism in New York. Five months ago he had returned to Ganae to act as press aide in Jeannot's presidential campaign.

I stood by his corpse, not in tears as Jeannot was, but sick, my mind filled with images of death: Mathieu, the corpse on the bonfire at Damienville, the mutilated body of Colonel Maurras in the college sacristy, the children hiding behind their dead parents in a Papanos ditch.

Ahead of us, the road was empty. Birds sang. Stormclouds scudded over the horizon. Large, heavy raindrops began to fall, warning of a downpour. We lifted Mathieu's body and put it on the floor in the back of the car. I used a rock to smash the rest of the windshield and remove it so that I could see to drive. Then, rain pelting in our faces, we went on. We were now only minutes from Cap Gauche, a rocky peninsula joined to the mainland by an isthmus. When we reached the causeway we saw a group of people walking across it, coming away from Cap Gauche. To our surprise some were carrying bedraggled posters bearing Jeannot's picture, holding them over their heads as shelter from the rain.

We drove on to the peninsula and came to the fishing town of Skele. The place seemed quiet, almost empty. There were no troops in sight. Jeannot, who remembered Skele from the time of his campaigning, gave me directions which led us to a hill above the harbour and a large Victorian gingerbread mansion with a widow's walk and a rounded turret from which a radio antenna poked up into the rain-drenched sky. As we drove up, a bearded man waved to us from the bay window of the mansion's front living room.

'That's Willi,' Jeannot said.

Willi Narodny, a bachelor in his fifties, was one of those adventurers who exile themselves from European society to live among the people of distant lands. Some years ago he had started a factory here, making baseball catcher's mitts, a factory which now employed half of the adult population of Cap Gauche. Through his ham radio station he promoted liberal and ecological causes. Now, shirtless, in cut-off jeans and hiking boots, he came hurrying out to meet us.

'Quick! Get out of the car and give me your car keys.'

We stared at him, uncomprehending.

'I just heard on the police radio that they're looking for a white Peugeot. They have the licence number.'

I handed him the keys. He got into the Peugeot and, as he did, saw what was in the back seat.

'Oh Jesus. Who is he?'

'A friend,' Jeannot said.

'Wait here. I'll hide the car in my garage.'

We watched him drive around to the rear of the big house. I looked at Jeannot.

'Are you still going to broadcast?'

'I hope so.'

Willi came hurrying up. 'Come inside.'

He led us into a crowded front room of the mansion. I saw a jumble of radio equipment similar to the transmission gear at Pat Redmond's place.

'Do you want a drink?'

We said no.

Willi went to a sideboard, took out a bottle of whisky and poured some into a glass. He drank, then asked, 'Did that happen on the road?'

'Yes. Some soldiers drove by, firing at random.'

'The Army's on the rampage all right,' Willi said. 'There's trouble everywhere.'

'What about Cap Gauche?' Jeannot asked. 'We saw some people crossing the causeway just now.'

'Those were fishermen from Bouglie. At noon today they staged a demonstration in the town.'

'Was there trouble?'

'No. The local garrison had sent its troops to Papanos, before the demo started. What are your plans, Jeannot? Do you still want to go on the air?'

'It's up to you. I want to let the people know I'm still here, still free.'

'And afterwards?'

'We'll leave right away.'

'You can't, not in that car. You'll be picked up. Where are you headed?'

We looked at each other.

'Maybe Lavallie,' Jeannot said. 'If we can get there.'

'Can either of you handle a motor bike?'

'I can,' I said.

'I have one. It's old but it works.'

'What about the broadcast?' Jeannot said. 'Is it possible?'

'Of course it's possible. But you'll have to keep it short. I'll tape it and air it later today and make sure it's also picked up abroad. By the time they trace it back—if they do—you'll be long gone.'

A few minutes later, Jeannot sat in front of a microphone in that crowded room overlooking the town of Skele. In front of him, a red lamp bulb switched to green.

Brothers and Sisters,

I speak to you from Ganae.

Yes, I am here.

I am still your priest. I am still your president.

Soon, I will speak to you again from Port Riche.

The plotters, the rich,

The generals, the old Doumerguists,

The *bleus* who have come out of hiding,

All will be punished and disgraced.

Today, on the orders of the criminal Macandal

Who has crept back into this country,

Soldiers are given bottles of *usque*.

They are told to get drunk.

And drunk, they are killing their brothers,

For what reason?

For no reason.

But yes, there is a reason,

A reason in the mind of General Macandal.

The reason is fear.

Fear is his weapon and he will use it.

He will use soldiers and guns to make you afraid.

If you are afraid, you will not rise up and demand
That freedom be given back to Ganae.
He is afraid.
He is afraid because you have gone into the streets,
To show that the freedom we have won is ours.
That we are not afraid of drunken soldiers,
That we are not afraid of murderers with guns.
We are millions.
They are few.
Already, their coup has failed.
People of Ganae,
Know your power.
Use it.
We will defend the election.
We will defend democracy.
Already, the great world has learned the truth.
Already, in the capitals of America and Europe,
These criminals have been denounced.
Their time is short.
Their day is done.
They have failed.
So go into the streets.
Rejoice.
You are the people.
You have the power.
Use it.

Jeannot looked up, signalling that he had finished. The green lamp switched to red.

'Too long?'

Willi shook his head. 'No. But tell me. Do you realise what you're saying?'

'What do you mean?'

'Go into the streets. Use your power. Last week they did that, didn't they? They used machetes and they got away with it. But things have changed. The Army's on the loose now. The Army has the guns. You're inviting a massacre.'

'If the people come out on the streets in full force, the Army can't shoot all of them, can they? They'd have to kill hundreds, maybe thousands. And by tomorrow Port Riche will be filled with foreign journalists.' He stood up, putting his hand on Willi's shoulder. 'This is what I want to say. I believe it will work. Will you send it?'

'OK, I made a promise,' Willi said. 'I don't like it, but I'll send it out an hour from now.'

'Thank you.'

Jeannot turned to me. 'What will we do about Mathieu?'

'The boy in your car?' Willi said. 'There's a priest here, Father Briand, a supporter of yours.'

'Yes, of course,' Jeannot said. 'He helped in my campaign.'

'I'll ask him to arrange the burial,' Willi said. He picked up the bottle again. 'Are you sure you won't have a drink?'

'I don't drink,' Jeannot said. 'Maybe Paul?'

I shook my head.

'Well, then.' Willi fumbled in his shorts pocket and handed me a key. 'Let's go and get the bike.'

A few minutes later we stood in his garage, as he wheeled an old motor bike out from the shadows. I looked back at our little white Peugeot, its windshield shattered, its doors pocked with bullet marks, Mathieu dead inside. I had not said a prayer for his soul. The familiar words came to mind. 'Eternal rest grant unto him, O Lord. And let perpetual light shine upon him.' But they were remembered, not said. Perpetual light? Eternal rest? My mother's words came back.

Willi was explaining the workings of the motor bike. He handed me a pair of goggles. To Jeannot he gave a visored helmet. 'Let Jeannot wear the helmet,' he said. 'I don't have two of them. But it's like a mask. He won't be recognised.'

I wheeled the bike out into the sunlight. Jeannot climbed on behind me. I kicked the engine into life. Willi waved to us.

Minutes later, we roared back across the causeway, the road empty, the rain ended. I looked down at Jeannot's hands clasped around my waist and felt his frail body press against mine. Back through the years, a woman sat on a ramshackle porch, watching, as I went down a hilly road on muleback, a little boy hanging on behind me, a boy she had given into my care.

We were headed for Lavallie where Noël Destouts had lent us his small cottage in the hills. The locals were mountain people, like the people of Toumalie, Jeannot's village. There were no *bleus* among them. If there was a place in Ganae where he might go to ground, Lavallie was that place.

But twenty minutes up the road, after crossing the causeway, we saw an army roadblock ahead. Vehicles and pedestrians were being checked by soldiers. Sober soldiers. The operation was being supervised by a captain wearing the shoulder flash of the Port Riche Battalion. I brought the motor bike to a stop.

'They'll be looking for your little white Peugeot,' Jeannot said. 'Not for two men on a motor bike.'

'They'll be looking for you and for a *blanc* priest. We can't risk it.'

'Is there another road to Lavallie?'

'No.'

I turned the bike round and we drove back the way we had come. As we approached the causeway, I saw that a second roadblock was being set up there. We were now cut off in both directions. A convoy of three army trucks was crossing the causeway, coming from Cap Gauche.

'Those trucks may have been to Willi's,' Jeannot said. 'One thing is sure. Someone back at Pat Redmond's place has given them that description of your car and told them we're in this area.'

Our danger had doubled. Before, we had been hiding. Now, we were hunted. As we halted in the middle of the road, the truck convoy rumbled through the roadblock. In a few minutes it would be on us. Hurriedly, we pulled the motor bike into the long grasses and lay down beside it, not knowing if we could be seen from the road. After a few moments we felt the ground shake as the trucks passed above us. I buried my head in the grass, cringing, as though at any moment a bullet would strike my back. When the sound diminished, Jeannot sat up, lifted the visor of his helmet and scanned the hills around us. He pointed to a village that stuck out on a rocky promontory overlooking the road and the valley below. 'Let's hide the bike and go up there.'

'But it's completely cut off,' I said. 'What will we do there?'

'That place is too small to have police or soldiers. The people will hide me.'

I didn't know what to say. I was afraid. I wanted to hide. I felt that at any moment we might be discovered by soldiers down here on the road. Yet if we went up that rocky path to that isolated place we would be cut off, on foot, unable to escape if pursued. We set off, pushing the heavy bike up the narrow path, looking for a place to hide it. Trees and bushes had long ago been razed for firewood and the bare mountain slopes offered no cover. We heard a noise above us. It grew louder. Coming over the mountaintop was a helicopter, a rare sight in Ganae. As it came towards us we saw its army markings. Hastily, we dragged the bike off the path and lay down beside it with little hope of not being seen. But the helicopter flew over us and did not pause. We watched it circle towards the second roadblock, hover, then lift up to disappear behind a hill.

'Missed us,' Jeannot said.

But I did not feel so sure.

'Let's leave the bike behind those rocks,' Jeannot said. 'At least it won't be seen from the road.'

We pulled the bike in behind some boulders. Jeannot put

his helmet down beside it. 'They *didn't* see us,' he said. 'Come on.'

He led. I followed. As we continued up the rocky path leading to the hilltop village, I kept glancing back at the road-block below. If the Army had learned that we were some-where between Cap Gauche and Papanos, they would send in hundreds of soldiers to flush us out. Pelardy was right. Jean-not, free in Ganae, was a man marked down for death.

The village ahead of us was of the poorest sort, some fif-teen wood-frame shacks, with walls of mud-daubed wattles, their roofs thatched with palm branches. On the steep slopes around them were a few mean fields of congo peas and yams. In the centre of the village we saw three hobbled donkeys, a pen containing a few pigs and, on the rocky bluffs above, six mountain goats. Now we heard the sound of drums and a *mandoline*. Voices chanted a dirge which I did not recognise. But Jeannot did.

'It's a wake,' he said. 'In that house.'

Children playing on a makeshift see-saw waved to us as we went to the open door of the shack Jeannot had pointed out. Inside, people were beating drums, clapping hands, and sing-ing to the sound of the *mandoline*. When they saw Jeannot they smiled and beckoned him to come in. But when we did and the singers saw my *blanc* face, their voices faltered. The music stopped.

The dead man was seated at a table dressed, as was the custom, in his best clothes, a clean white shirt, denim trou-sers, sandals. His old felt fedora was perched jauntily on his head. On the table was a funerary wreath fashioned from white frangipani and red immortelles. A dish of plantains, beans and rice had been set before him and an unlit cigarette drooped from his lips. He was a peasant in his thirties, scare-crow thin, as were most of the others in the room. And then I saw the bullet hole in his temple. The blood had been cleaned away.

People nodded humbly to me, the priest. They looked with curiosity at Jeannot, not recognising him.

Jeannot smiled at them and said, 'God is with us.'

It was as though he had spoken his name. There was, at once, an amazing stillness in the room. In a chorus, voices answered.

'*C'e Mesiah. C'e Mesiah!*'

People came forward touching him as they might touch a sacred object. '*Mesiah! Mesiah!*' They wept, they smiled, they bowed to him in reverence.

Jeannot, moving through the crowd, went to the table and gently touched the dead man's hand.

'Who killed our brother?'

Stumbling, interrupting each other in their eagerness to tell, the villagers explained that they had gone down to Papanos two days ago to join other peasants in a protest against parliament's refusal to accept Jeannot's choice of premier. The dead man was carrying a poster with Jeannot's picture and had been shot by soldiers when he tried to hoist it up over the entrance to the town hall.

And now, as in a biblical miracle, Jeannot had appeared at the dead man's wake. The villagers did not ask why he had come or how he knew of the death. The Messiah is not a man. He co-exists in the world of the flesh and the world of the spirit. To them, Jeannot had appeared in their village as the Virgin might appear. He was God's messenger. Because of this, the room was filled with a strange exaltation. These lives of poverty, of endless toil, of children's early deaths, of storms that washed away the meagre crops, of soldiers and *bleus* who beat and pillaged, were, in that room, on that day, transformed into the promise of a future life. Now, with the Messiah come among them, they believed anew. Paradise would be theirs.

In that moment their gratitude was moving, awkward and intense. Women came forward with bowls of food, pushing it into our hands. Men poured cups of homemade beer and brought them to Jeannot, smiling shyly as they tried to force him to drink. We were seated at the table with the dead man, and offered precious cigarettes. Our sandals were removed and the village women brought water to wash our muddied feet. And now the drums began to beat again, the *mandoline* twanged to a more lively tune. The wake resumed, but all was changed: life had vanquished death. The corpse, stiff and silent at the table, would rejoin us one day in another, truer world.

We were hunted men. On the roads below us and in the sky, soldiers were searching for Jeannot. And yet in that room it was as though we had been rescued from our enemies. We ate the food given us and clapped our hands, as the villagers sang in celebration. I did not ask Jeannot what we should do next. But in the midst of the singing he said to me, 'These people may not even know there's been a coup. They say they have no radio here.'

'Will you tell them?'

'Later. Perhaps they know some place, higher up the mountain, where we might hide for a day or two.'

Just then, a very old woman was led up to meet Jeannot. She was the dead man's grandmother. Jeannot embraced her and said, 'He is in heaven now. He is happy.'

'I know,' the old woman said. 'He make a lot of mistakes in his time, but he stood for you last week in the town. That buys him his ticket to paradise. Eh, Jeannot?'

He smiled and embraced her again. A few minutes later, over the singing and the drums, we heard the clatter of helicopter propellers. The helicopter circled the huts of the village, hovered, then tilted up and moved off down the mountainside. People who had run out to look came back into the room. 'Soldiers! Soldiers coming!'

'Stay here,' I told Jeannot. I went out of the hut. A long

line of soldiers was advancing up the mountainside, spread out as in a military exercise. On the bluffs behind the village other soldiers were crouched, rifles at the ready. The helicopter came back, hovered stationary above us, then moved down to the road where a dozen army trucks and two weapons carriers were parked in convoy.

I ran back into the room and told Jeannot.

'You were right,' he said. 'They saw us with the motor bike. They know we're here.'

Villagers came crowding around him. 'Soldiers coming, Jeannot. What do they want?'

'They want me,' Jeannot said. He took my arm. 'If they take me, they won't care about you. Let's see if we can find somewhere for you to hide.'

'No. We'll stay together.'

Now we heard the sound of gunfire. We ran out. The soldiers, coming up the mountain, were firing their rifles in the air to frighten the villagers who stood staring down at them. When the rifles went off, some of the people crowded back behind the huts. But one woman shouted, 'They come for Jeannot. They going to shoot him!'

At that, in a sudden shift of mood, the crowd grew angry. Some ran into their huts and reemerged with machetes. The first soldiers were now only a hundred yards away. When they saw the villagers come out with machetes, they hesitated and looked at their officer, a lieutenant, who was coming up beside them. 'Go on!' he shouted. 'Go on! They have no guns.'

The soldiers, closer now, again raised their guns and fired over the villagers' heads. The villagers stood their ground. The soldiers advanced. The officer shouted, 'Open fire!'

They fired into the crowd. Two men fell. A woman, bleeding from a wound in her shoulder, ran forward screaming wordlessly at the attackers.

Jeannot, standing beside me, pushed past his defenders,

stepping in front of the villagers. The officer, recognising him, hastily called out, 'Hold your fire!'

Jeannot walked a few paces towards the soldiers, then stopped. He raised his hands in a gesture of truce. Suddenly, all was quiet. He spoke in a normal tone.

'Brothers, put down your guns. Do not kill your own people. I am here. Put down your guns.'

He stood, alone, a slight, frail, shabby figure, yet, as always when he wished it, commanding absolute attention. The soldiers lowered their guns. In the silence we heard the crunch of boots on the rocky path as a captain came up to join the Lieutenant. Both were *mulâtres* and wore the shoulder flash of the Port Riche Battalion. The Captain drew his pistol and pointed it at Jeannot.

'You are under arrest, Father Cantave.'

'You must leave these people in peace,' Jeannot said. 'They have nothing to do with me.'

He walked towards the officers. I followed him. When he reached the officers, he turned and called back to the villagers.

'Put away your machetes. Help those who are injured. Go in. Go in.'

His voice broke. He said, 'God bless you.'

He turned to the officers. 'I am the one you want. Let Father Michel go home.'

The officer shook his head. 'I have orders,' he said. 'I must bring him in.'

We started down the path in single file, followed by the Captain and the Lieutenant. The soldiers remained spread out uncertainly on the mountainside until a sergeant called, 'Return to transport. Return to transport.'

I looked up. The villagers were watching us, their machetes slack in their hands. Some of them knelt by the two who had been shot. When we reached the road Jeannot turned and waved to them. From far off, their voices came down the mountainside, singing 'Dieu et Patrie.'

Soldiers going back to their trucks passed by us on the crowded road. I saw them stare at Jeannot with a mixture of awe and curiosity. Some smiled and waved to him, as to a friend. The Captain, noticing this, spoke to a sergeant. The Sergeant came up to us, gesturing with his Uzi, pointing in the direction we should take. The army helicopter was parked further down the road. When we reached it, the pilot leaned over to help us climb into the machine. The Captain and the Lieutenant also boarded. The Captain spoke to the pilot and at once the rotary blades began their deafening merry-go-round. We lifted off and tilted over the mountaintop. Below, the villagers of that unknown village looked up at us. They had seen their Messiah. Two of them may have died for him.

It was now late afternoon and, as the helicopter clattered over the hills, tropical rain drenched the plastic walls that enclosed us. The Captain, sitting opposite Jeannot, reached forward and plucked the pocket radio from Jeannot's shirt pocket. 'Not allowed,' he shouted.

I noticed that the young Lieutenant kept staring at me. At last, leaning towards me, he shouted in my ear, 'Do you know me, Father? Sami, Henri Sami. I was a student of yours. Yes! At the college.'

I did not remember him but I knew his family name. The Samis were among the richest of the *mulâtre* elite.

'Where are we going?' I asked him.

'There.' He pointed ahead. Through the rain-cleared space caused by the pilot's windshield wipers, I saw, below us, a fort, set in a rocky plain and surrounded by high stone walls. The Ganaen flag flew from a turret in the courtyard. As we landed in that courtyard in a rush of propeller backdraft, the rain had slackened to a drizzle. A sign above the main gate read:

ARMÉE DE GANAE
CAP BELLE ISLE
ÉTAT MAJOR

The fort seemed deserted. When we got out of the helicopter the windows on each floor were shuttered. The ground-floor doors were closed. A soldier, waving landing batons, was our only welcomer. The Captain and Lieutenant Sami jumped down and looked around them uncertainly. One of the doors opened. A major emerged and came up to us. Our escorts saluted him. We were led through the opened door of the fort into a darkened corridor and then into a room. No one spoke. The Major nodded to the others and all three went out, leaving Jeannot and me alone. We heard them lock the door. Jeannot seated himself in one of six chairs which were arranged around a plain wooden table. The room was without any other furniture. On the wall was a blackboard which had been scrubbed clean.

'The broadcast,' he said. 'Willi said he would send it "in an hour." What time is it now?'

I looked at my watch. 'Five o'clock.'

'If it went out at one and was picked up, people may already be in the streets.'

There were no lights on in the room. As it grew darker I found a switch but it did not work. Towards six we heard a bell ring in the corridor. Minutes later, floodlights were switched on in the courtyard outside. We went to the window and saw the soldier who had guided our helicopter down standing in the middle of the yard. His red landing batons were now illuminated. He waited. We waited. Above, growing louder, we heard the sound of a helicopter. The soldier guided it to a landing some twenty yards away from the helicopter that had brought us to this place. In the floodlights it was highly visible.

'See the decal?' Jeannot said. 'Three stars. That's Hemon's helicopter.'

But when the helicopter door opened and an officer appeared it was not General Hemon. This officer was light-skinned, very tall, wearing combat uniform and the insignia of a four-star general, the only such ranking in the Ganaen Army. As he turned around, the Major, who had come into the glare of the floodlights, saluted him with punctilio. General Macandal acknowledged the salute. Behind him, vaulting down easily from the helicopter, was Colonel Lambert. I recognised him at once; his handsome face, his dashing manner, the flamboyant, film-star moustache. He too wore combat gear, pressed, neat, unused in battle. The Army of Ganae has never fought a war.

Preceded by the Major, the General and Lambert walked towards our building. As we watched from our darkened room, the room light came on. We heard a bell ring in the corridor outside and the shuffle of soldiers' boots on stone floors. Our enemies approached. I felt a sudden panic: the barracks had become a prison from which we would never come out alive.

A key turned in the door. General Macandal and Colonel Lambert entered the room. The Major pulled the door shut again, leaving us alone.

Jeannot did not rise from his chair, nor did he speak. General Macandal, tall, towering over Jeannot, his face a mask of contempt, turned to Lambert. 'Get rid of the priest. We will talk to him alone.'

'Father Michel stays here,' Jeannot said.

The General looked at him. 'You are no longer in charge. A state of martial law is now in effect.'

'I will not talk to you or to anyone unless Father Michel is present as my witness,' Jeannot said.

The General sat down at the other end of the table. 'All right, let him stay,' he said to Lambert.

Lambert sat, straddling a chair, his legs thrust out. He turned, looked at me, and smiled in a friendly manner.

'What is this talk of martial law?' Jeannot said.

'You have been here all afternoon,' the General said. 'So, of course you have no idea of the damage you have done. I have been forced to declare martial law because of the speech you broadcast earlier today. I hope it will be a temporary measure. That depends on you.'

'So the people are back in the streets,' Jeannot said. 'And your coup has failed.'

'Listen to me!' the General said. 'In the last two hours crowds of looters and rioters have been running wild in Port Riche, Mele, Doumergueville and Papanos. In the rural regions the peasants have burned down property and threatened the lives of soldiers, police and elected officials. We don't yet know how many people have been killed. I have ordered the Army not to retaliate, but in some cases these orders have been disobeyed. I hold you responsible for these events.'

'Nonsense,' Jeannot said. 'You engineered this coup. You are responsible for everything that has happened.'

'*You* are responsible,' the General said. 'The truth is, you have never wanted democracy for Ganae. You have tried to foment a revolution, a war of the poor *noirs* against the rest of us. You pretend to be a priest but you are not a priest, you are a revolutionary, preaching class warfare. You are not fit to govern Ganae. That is why Senator Raymond has become premier. Parliament is trying to save this country from a civil war which you are attempting to provoke. If that happens, the country will be destroyed. I am offering you a compromise. We have decided we will allow you to remain as president under certain conditions. Do you wish to hear them?'

'Where is General Hemon?' Jeannot said.

The General sighed and stared at the ceiling. 'Will you stop all this nonsense! Listen to me! These are the conditions under which we will allow you to remain as president. You will be taken tonight to Radio Libre. There will be journalists present. You will tell them that you have come there to broadcast an appeal for an end to this violence. We will then broadcast a taped speech, made by you, in which you announce that you concur in parliament's decision to appoint Senator Raymond as premier. You will say that you accept this as a measure to try to restore order and peace in Ganae. You will explain that you now wish to share power with the premier and with parliament. I would suggest that you end with a prayer for peace.'

'And how do you propose to make me do this?' Jeannot asked.

'You will do it because it is in your interest to co-operate with us.'

'You haven't answered my question,' Jeannot said.

'What will happen if you don't co-operate? You will disappear. You may have fled the country, you may be in hiding, you may have been killed. Your followers will attempt to locate you. There will be the usual conspiracy theories but nothing will be proven. The OAS will announce that you are still the elected president of Ganae, but that you have vanished. After some months, when there is no new information, the world's attention tends to move elsewhere. A new president will be elected and you will pass into history. I was Chief of Staff in the days of President Doumergue. I know how these things end.'

There was silence in the room. Colonel Lambert produced a silver cigarette case and offered cigarettes to me and to the General. No one accepted. Lambert then lit a cigarette and spoke for the first time.

'So, Father Cantave. You are an intelligent man and the General is offering you a fair choice. We are asking you to help end this bloodshed and save many lives. If you do it, you will remain as president of Ganae. If you don't, we will govern without you. It's up to you.'

I looked at Jeannot. At the beginning of this interview he had been outraged. Now he seemed unsure. He put his hand up, shielding his eyes, as though he were in pain. At last, he said, 'I can't go on radio tonight. I must have time to think about this.'

The General turned to Lambert. 'Alain?'

'The curfew is in effect until eight o'clock tomorrow morning,' Lambert said. 'The storm will dampen things down in most parts of the island. Supposing I ring Father Cantave at ten o'clock tonight? That should give him time to make up his mind.'

'Father Cantave?' The General stared at Jeannot.

For a moment Jeannot did not answer him or look at him. At last, he said, 'I will talk to you at ten.'

'Good,' the General said. He turned back to Lambert. 'Now, what about the others? Have you heard from the Archbishop?'

'Yes. He's promised to speak on radio and television at nine o'clock tonight. There will be prayers for the healing of Ganae's wounds. Senator Raymond will also take part in the broadcast.'

Outside, it began to rain again, a downpour that washed the windows of the room we were in, as though someone had turned a hose on the glass. General Macandal looked up at the sound, then asked Lambert, 'Was there a hurricane warning, do you know?'

'I think it's called Dominic,' Lambert said. 'It's moving up from Barbados.'

'We'd better get back to Port Riche then,' the General said. 'I've set up an eight o'clock meeting with the American Ambassador.'

They spoke easily, conversationally, as though Jeannot and I were no longer in the room. There was something more chilling in this insouciance than in their former words of menace. The General rose from the table, put on his forage cap and said, 'Ready, Alain?'

Lambert turned to me. 'Father Michel, my wife is coming home tomorrow. She managed to telephone me this morning as soon as she heard I had returned. She told me of your kindness to her. Thank you. We are in your debt.'

He and General Macandal walked out of the room. The Major appeared in the doorway.

'Come with me.'

He led us down the dark corridor and up a flight of barracks stairs. Above, I heard the sound of the helicopter as it lifted into the sky. We were led into a small room with two beds and two sinks. 'We will bring you some supper in a while,' the Major said. 'Colonel Lambert will ring you at ten o'clock.'

He shut the door. Jeannot went at once and lay down on the bed, covering his eyes with his hand.

'Migraine?'

'It will pass. Just let me lie quietly for a little. Can we put the light out?'

And so I sat on the other bed in darkness. Outside, the storm beat on the window. I watched Jeannot who lay face down, unmoving. What would I do if I were him? In the past twelve hours I had seen violent and senseless death more often than at any time in my life. He had seen it too and yet, when he went on radio, he had not tried to stop it. Was he still certain that his actions were God's will?

An hour later there was a knock on the door. This time it was Lieutenant Sami, accompanied by a soldier who brought us coffee and a dish of eggs and bread.

'Why are you here in the dark?' Sami asked, switching on the light.

'Turn it off,' I said.

'No, it's all right.' Jeannot sat up in the bed. I saw that he was sweating, his face drained, his eyes clouded. 'Are you listening to the radio?' he asked Sami. 'Is there still trouble in the streets?'

'Things are quieter now,' Sami said. 'It's the hurricane. It's hit Mele. They say it will bypass the rest of the island but it's raining everywhere. You know that there's a curfew, don't you? People will be shot if they go out in the streets.'

'Yes, we know. Thank you,' Jeannot said.

When Sami and the soldier left the room, Jeannot said, 'They can't turn the clock back, can they? People took to the streets today, thousands of them. We're winning. What do you think?'

'You say we're winning. The world is on our side. But you said, earlier, that the Army has taken over, that the Army is now the law. What protection will our people have against armed soldiers? You say it's too late for Macandal and Lambert to turn the clock back. But what about those who've died already, what about the others who will die tomorrow and the next day and the next? They can't turn the clock back either.'

He looked at me with pain-clouded eyes. 'If there are enough of us, if our will is strong, it won't last long. But the question I ask myself is this. If I refuse them and they shoot me tonight, will the people carry on without me? Macandal is lying when he says he'd pretend I'd disappeared. He'd hang my corpse on a lamppost in the Avenue de la République to prove that I'm no longer a danger. And then what will people do? That's what I must think of now.'

He bent his head, his hand over his eyes. 'Do you mind if we put out the light for a while? And not talk?'

I switched off the light. Fifteen minutes later it was switched on again. The Major stood in the doorway. 'Colonel Lambert is on the telephone. Come.'

Jeannot left and was gone for half an hour. When he came back he went to the sink, washed his face and wiped it with a towel. He seemed alert, his old self.

'What happened?'

'I told Lambert I will remain as president and accept Raymond as my premier. I will speak on Radio Libre tomorrow morning but I insisted that it be live and that I be seen on television. The people must see me, they must know I'm still here, still in charge. I have also promised to hold a press conference and reassure the foreign journalists.'

At that moment I felt a strange sense of relief. 'Good,' I said. 'I think you've made a wise decision.'

'I didn't make a decision. I prayed to God for an answer. He has given me an answer I could not have dreamed of.'

'Tell me.'

He shook his head. 'I can't. God has decided this game. Tomorrow, we will play it out. Now, try to get some sleep.'

TEN

SOMETHING HAPPENED that night. I woke to the sound of truck engines starting up in the courtyard below. Floodlights had been switched on and their reflection silvered the darkness of our room. I heard the sound of soldiers' boots, voices shouting orders and the slamming of tailboards as the vehicles moved out. I got up and went to the window. Below, a dozen trucks filled with armed soldiers were moving in convoy through the main gates of the fort. When they had gone, a lone soldier crossed the courtyard to close the gates behind them. I looked back at Jeannot. He lay on the bed, his hands crossed on his chest, his eyes open, staring at the ceiling, immobile as the funerary statue of a medieval knight, recumbent on a tombstone. Below, the noise died to silence. The courtyard lights were shut off. His profile became a silhouette. It did not move. I stared at it. I was watching someone I did not know.

Shortly after dawn, Lieutenant Sami unlocked the door to admit a soldier who brought us coffee, bread and bananas. Sami said we would be leaving for Port Riche in half an hour. But minutes after he left the room the helicopter in the courtyard below began to rev up its rotary blades. The Major appeared.

'I'm sorry, but we must hurry. Are you ready?'

Outside, the rains had ended. A rust-coloured dawn faded to the monotonous blue of a Ganaen summer's day. Lieutenant Sami shook hands with me just before I boarded the helicopter, saying, 'Some day I must come and visit you at the college, Father. Those were happy times for me. Good luck on your journey.'

Jeannot was already in the helicopter. The Major, who sat directly behind us, took his revolver from its holster and held it slack on his lap. We flew high over the desolate plain that surrounded the fort. Within minutes we came to the coastline, a white rim of breakers far below us. In the noise of the engines I could barely hear the pilot's voice on the intercom but I caught the words. 'ETA seven-twenty-seven . . . Escort?'

Suddenly, on our left, two small army training planes flew alongside, then climbed above us. Our pilot turned and shouted back to the Major, 'All clear. All clear. We can go in.'

The Major nodded and leaned forward, shouting in Jeannot's ear. 'We'll be landing soon.'

The helicopter banked and turned towards the sea. Ahead, we saw the sprawl of Port Riche, the docks, the deserted exhibition grounds, the gleaming white shell of the presidential palace. As we came lower, the streets seemed empty. It was not yet eight. The curfew was still in effect. Soldiers were stationed at all the major crossroads and a cluster of army vehicles was parked in the Place Mafoux, a few streets away from the palace. Now we were over Radio Libre with its high, barbed-wire fences, its antenna, and, in the car-park, some thirty armed soldiers. Clouds of dust billowed across the steps of the front entrance as the helicopter settled down near a group of official limousines. When the dust cleared and we climbed out of the helicopter, six soldiers surrounded Jeannot, like a bodyguard. Some yards away I saw a dozen foreign journalists and as many photographers, who were being held back from approaching us.

On the steps of the radio station, Colonel Lambert, in uniform, a revolver holstered on his belt, beckoned the soldiers to bring Jeannot inside, then smiling at the foreign journalists, called out in English over the noise of the helicopter, 'All right, gentlemen, all right. In a moment, in a moment.'

From the main hallway of the radio station, we were taken quickly into a small room. Lambert preceded us, accompanied by two civilians. Jeannot's military escort remained outside. The two men who came into the room with Lambert wore dark suits, white shirts, and black ties. They were large, heavily-built *mulâtres*, sullen and tense, as though at any moment they might be called on to do something violent. Although he kept smiling, I could see that Lambert was also tense. He said to Jeannot, 'Father Cantave, everything has been arranged as you wished. Your address will be carried live on both television and radio. There has been one hitch, which is that the foreign press wants to interview you before you make your address. I know you didn't want that. But I would be grateful if you would tell them yourself.'

'Of course,' Jeannot said. 'Let them in. I'll speak to them now.'

'One moment,' Lambert said. 'We have made an agreement and I intend to live up to my part of the bargain. Just remember that I control the facilities of Radio Libre this morning. If I hear something which negates our bargain, your address will be terminated at once.'

'I would have expected as much,' Jeannot said. 'I don't think you'll have to worry about that.' He turned and stared at the two dark-suited strangers. 'Who are these men?'

Lambert smiled. 'Your guardian angels. It's just for today. Shall I bring the press in?'

'Yes.'

They came in, in a rush, the photographers at once snapping pictures, the reporters crowding forward, the questions overlapping. 'Would you say this was a coup—have you been ill-treated—is it true that you've been replaced?' I recognised most of them as regulars at the bar of the Hotel Régence, resident correspondents for their national newspapers and networks, and, thus, well briefed on recent events. Jeannot held up his hands, silent until the noise subsided.

'Gentlemen, I am about to make a public address. It will be on television and radio and I think it will answer your questions. Other than that I am not prepared to discuss the events of the past twenty-four hours. I hope that what I tell the people will help to arrest this tragic chain of events. That is all, gentlemen.'

'Why is there blood on your shirt?' someone called out. 'Were you injured—were you attacked?'

'It's not my blood,' Jeannot said. 'It is the blood of my friend Mathieu Clément who was killed yesterday in a tragic accident. I have not been attacked.'

He turned to Lambert. 'All right. Let's go.'

The two dark-suited men at once cleared a passage for us through the reporters and photographers. In the corridor we were surrounded by the six armed soldiers who led us at a brisk pace up a flight of stairs and into a suite of offices and studios. An elderly, elegant man, smelling strongly of scent, came forward, welcoming Jeannot like an old friend. 'Good to see you, Monsieur le Président. Everything's ready for the broadcast. Do you want to go straight in?'

'Come with me,' Jeannot said, taking my arm. The two dark-suited men closed in on either side of us as we entered a hangar-like space which was a television studio. Lambert followed. A make-up man in a white smock came over to Jeannot. 'Sir, will we change your shirt?' Jeannot shook his head.

The floor director came up and shook hands with him. Jeannot was familiar to these people, at home in this atmosphere. In the days of his campaign and his presidency Radio Libre was a place he visited every other day. Now he went up to the broadcast area and sat in an armchair. Technicians moved around him. A small microphone was attached to the collar of his dirty white shirt. The two dark-suited men stood a little off to the side and, as one of them eased his heavy buttocks against a wall, I saw the bulge of a revolver under his armpit. Lambert, who whispered something to the elegant old station manager, came into the broadcast area and stood off-camera, a little to the left of Jeannot. He raised his hand and made some signal to the dark-suited thugs. They nodded. Lights glared down on Jeannot. A television camera moved in on him. The floor manager waved to Jeannot and pointed to a clock. A young announcer stepped up to the microphone on Jeannot's left. He watched the clock. When the hand touched eight, the camera rolled towards him and he spoke.

'This is Radio Libre. This is a special broadcast on national television and radio. We have with us here in our studio Father Jean-Paul Cantave, President of Ganae. President Cantave.'

I looked at Jeannot and saw that he no longer sat in the armchair but had risen and stood facing the cameras. I looked at the monitor and saw that he was in close-up, his eyes staring trancelike at his unseen audience.

Brothers and Sisters,
Today, I weep.
I weep when I see our people shot dead in La Rotonde.
I weep when I see innocent farmers
Murdered in a ditch in Papanos.
I weep when I see a rich man and his family
Hacked to death in the square in Doumergueville.
I weep when I see the soldiers of Ganae,
Loosed like police dogs on the poor.
I weep because words of mine,

Yes, words which I spoke
Yesterday,
And the day before
And the day before that,
Words of mine may have sent
My Brothers and Sisters
To their deaths.
Words of mine may have sent
Soldiers into the streets of our cities
To kill and be killed.
And for what?
We have not won our freedom.
That is a long fight.
I know now
It will not happen today or tomorrow.
But it will happen.
It will happen when the people become one.
So strong, so loving that our enemies will fail.
The power of love is greater than the power of hate.
We must love our enemies
As Christ taught us to.
Even those who would rule us
By the gun and by fear.
They are our Brothers and Sisters.
We are one family. God's family.
I have been asked to stop this killing.
I have been asked by General Macandal
And by the parliament of Ganae
To appoint Senator Raymond as my premier.
I have been asked to share the powers you gave me
With others I did not choose.
Will I do this?

He paused. At once, in the studio, there was an air of
alarm. I saw the dark-suited thugs come to the alert. Lambert,

staring at Jeannot, raised his hand, signalling to the floor director, ready to halt the broadcast.

Jeannot kept staring at the camera. And then he said,

I will do it.
Yes.
I will do it because
Love drives out hate.
General Macandal,
You have asked me to conclude this address
With a prayer for peace in Ganae.
I will do more than that.
I ask you, Brothers and Sisters,
Here in this city
And in all the towns and villages of our land.
It is eight o'clock in the morning.
I ask
That in two hours' time we in Port Riche
Gather in the Place Notre Dame,
Before the Cathedral of Notre Dame de Secours.
As you, all over Ganae,
Must gather outside your churches
To pray.
To pray to Our Father that He help us now.
That He lead us to the freedom promised us.
We must ask His guidance
To end our troubles
To give us justice.
For the poor, the despised, the wretched.
Come.
Come in your thousands.
This morning, let us pray.

He bowed his head and joined his hands in an attitude of prayer, then looked off camera, signalling that he had finished his speech.

The cameras moved to the young announcer, who said, 'That was an address by President Jean-Paul Cantave, from our studios in Port Riche.'

In the background I heard the recorded music of the national anthem. Lambert went up to Jeannot who stood patiently, as crew members removed his microphone.

'That was very moving,' Lambert said. 'Excellent. I have just one question, however. This prayer service. What will it consist of?'

'We will say the rosary. That's all. The service will not be held inside the cathedral. I hope we will have too great a crowd for that. I also hope that, as this is a religious service, there will be no military presence in the Place Notre Dame.'

Lambert smiled and shook his head. 'I'm sorry, but in the present state of unrest an assembly of this size will have to be policed.'

'Peacefully,' Jeannot said. 'That's all I ask.'

'We will issue instructions. The military will behave. You have my word.'

The elegant old station manager came up self-importantly. 'Colonel, General Macandal is on the line.'

'Excuse me one moment,' Lambert said. He went off with the station manager.

Jeannot came over to me. 'Let's go back to the palace, Paul.'

One of the dark-suited thugs held up his hand: 'We must wait for the Colonel, sir.'

'Then let us wait,' Jeannot said. He smiled at me. 'This is the era of co-operation.'

So, we waited. After a few minutes, Lambert returned. 'General Macandal sends his compliments. He too, was pleased with what you have just said. He agrees with me, though, that we must have some policing presence at this rosary ceremony. He also suggests that Archbishop Pellerat be invited to take part in the service.'

'The Archbishop is welcome to attend, if he wishes,' Jeannot said. 'As I said, it will not be a service, but a simple recitation of the rosary. I will lead the prayers and we will need microphones set up in the square so that the congregation can follow them. And now, I would like to go back to the palace.'

'Of course. My men will drive you.' Lambert turned and pointed to the thugs. 'They will also take you to the service when the time comes.'

Jeannot looked at me. 'Ready, Paul?'

'Excuse me,' Lambert said. 'May I suggest that you won't be bothered by the press if you leave by the back entrance. It's up to you.'

'Good. I don't want any more questions.'

The station manager unlocked the small door and we were led through a yard, filled with rusting radio equipment. A black Mercedes waited. The dark-suited thugs then drove us out on to Rue Madame Ponset. The curfew had ended and the streets were busy with people. But it was far from a normal morning. There was an air of danger, excitement and disruption. No one seemed to be at work. As we drove through the market area, crowds were assembling and moving on foot and on bicycles in the direction of the Place Notre Dame. Some of these people held aloft placards bearing Jeannot's picture. Two women carried a long, sheet-like banner behind which some forty people marched as in a procession. The banner read: JEANNOT, LIBÉRATEUR!

When we drove into the palace courtyard an officer of the Garde Présidentielle met us at the main entrance. Jeannot turned to the dark-suited thugs. 'I am going up to my private quarters. I will come back down at nine-fifteen and you can drive me to the cathedral.'

'Is there more than one exit from his private rooms?' the thug asked the officer.

'No.'

'Good. We will come with you, sir, and wait outside your door until you are ready to leave for the service.'

To reach the presidential apartments we had to pass the suite of offices that house the President's staff. Those offices, once filled with Jeannot's advisers, helpers and handlers, were empty, the telephones silent, the computers switched off. The corridors where politicians, office-seekers and supplicants had waited to speak to the President, echoed to the lonely tramp of two soldiers of the guard. As we went towards the stairs that led to Jeannot's quarters, Sister Maria came hurrying down to meet us. 'Are you hurt?' she asked, pointing to his bloodied shirt.

'Where is everyone?' Jeannot asked.

'At home. Hiding. Until we heard you on the radio this morning we thought it was a coup.'

'It was.'

'Can I get you something? Are you wounded?'

'No, no. Ask Matta to bring us up some coffee. And, please, come to the rosary at ten.'

'Of course I will.' She shook her head. 'It was awful. I thought you were dead.'

The dark-suited men who had hung back during this conversation followed on our heels as we climbed the flights of marble stairs. At the top flight, sitting outside the doors to Jeannot's apartments, the middle-aged sergeants who had guarded him in the early days of his presidency rose and saluted. The dark-suited men nodded to them, but did not attempt to follow when the sergeants unlocked the heavy doors to admit us. Now, at last, I was alone with him. He went into the ornate bathroom, stripped off his shirt and began to wash. I followed him in, my mind confused with questions.

'What are you going to do?' I asked him. 'What's this about the rosary?'

'We will say the rosary. We will pray for God's help in bringing us the democracy we asked for.'

We heard sounds in the other room. Matta, a palace servant, entered with coffee. He called in to Jeannot, 'God bless you, you back with us.'

When Matta had gone I asked, 'What if Raymond and the parliament try to maintain the status quo? Raymond will never go against the Army. And Lambert is back. Aren't you worried about all of this?'

He came out of the bathroom and went into the huge bedroom where he took a white peasant shirt from a drawer. 'Of course I am. We'll never have freedom if those who lead the people don't work for the people. Raymond and the Army will work hand in hand against them.'

'And so?'

'Ganae has always been ruled by corrupt presidents, or by dictators. The people have always waited to be led. They must not rely on a leader. They must learn to make the revolution themselves.'

'But how can they do that?'

'Christ was a leader who did not lead,' Jeannot said.

'I don't understand you.'

'You will. Drink your coffee. We must go.'

In Ganae, white is the colour of pomp and power. The palace is white, the parliament buildings are white and Notre Dame de Secours, which is by far the largest religious edifice, is a blindingly white, Spanish-style cathedral built in the eighteenth century to overlook what was then the largest place of public assembly in the capital, the Place Notre Dame. Because the square is laid out in uneven, eighteenth-century cobblestones it is largely avoided by motor vehicles. It is a square for strollers, surrounded in the daytime by market stalls and, at night, lit by old-fashioned gas lamps, a meeting place for the youth of Port Riche.

In front of the cathedral, four impressive rows of stone steps lead down to the square. Three huge marble statues look out on the city: Christ, dying on the Cross; a blessed Virgin; a stern and bearded Saint Peter. The features of these statues are, like their colour, white. Perhaps because of the cathedral, the Place Notre Dame has never been the site of public demonstrations. It is, traditionally, a place of religious devotion and processions, a place where, after funerals, mourners kneel in front of the monumental statues to pray for the souls of their dead.

As Lambert's black-suited watchdogs drove our Mercedes towards the area, we were slowed to walking pace by the crowds converging on the square. The thugs, impatiently, began to sound the horn but Jeannot told them to be quiet. 'Do you want this car to be mobbed?' he said to them. 'If they see me, the people will not let us through.'

When he had said that, he sat with his head down, his hands covering his face as, slowly, we gained access to the square. At once, I saw a crowd larger than any I had ever seen assembled there. Police, arm-linked in double lines, had cleared an aisle for the cars of dignitaries. An army truck was positioned at each of the four entrances to the square but the military presence seemed negligible. Slowly, bumping and lurching, we drove over the uneven cobblestones and reached the front steps of the cathedral. Waiting on these steps were a contingent of the elite, several high army officers and their wives, leading parliamentarians, and a group of robed clerics. I did not see the Archbishop among them, but Bishop Laval, under whose jurisdiction the cathedral lay, came down the steps to welcome Jeannot. Father Bourque, Noël Destouts and others from our college were also present and as we climbed the steps towards the microphones and the podium, a group of Jeannot's 'liberation theology' priests and nuns surrounded him, besieging him with questions. I heard him ask about the microphones. The sacristans of the cathedral had set up loudspeakers which were used when the cathedral could not accommodate the crowds at a large ceremony. The prayers would be heard all over the huge square and broad-cast to the rest of the country.

A hand touched my shoulder. At first I did not recognise this stranger, dressed as for a fashionable wedding.

'Father Michel! I was hoping I'd see you here. I'll never forget your kindness to me. Oh—by the way—Reverend Mother sends her best wishes.'

I remembered the maddened crowds outside Fort Noël calling for her punishment. I looked down at the thousands of peasants and slum-dwellers assembled under the morning sun. Had they seen her? What would they do if they recognised her?

'Isn't it dangerous for you to be here, Madame?'

'I have my husband,' she said. 'With him, I never feel afraid. Besides, we are here to pray for peace, aren't we?'

Behind her, Lambert smiled at me. Behind Lambert I saw six soldiers of the Port Riche Battalion, facing out, watching the square, their Uzis at the ready. At that moment, Bishop Laval came up to me and shook hands. 'It's a little after ten. When do we begin? And have you ever seen such a crowd?'

'I'll ask Jeannot.'

I made my way through the clerics and dignitaries on the steps until I reached the bank of microphones where Jeannot stood. He was with Pelardy. Pelardy looked grim and displeased and, as I came up to them, I saw why. Senator Raymond, a portly figure in a double-breasted white suit, eyes opaque behind the gleaming lenses of aviator glasses, stood with his arm around Jeannot's shoulders while photographers snapped pictures. Jeannot did not return the embrace, but did not spurn it, remaining immobile, withdrawn.

'The Bishop is asking when do we begin,' I said.

'Is the General here?' Jeannot asked.

'The General is over there,' Raymond said, pointing to the main doors of the cathedral where, surrounded by his military aides, General Macandal stood in full dress uniform with a gold lanyard on his shoulder and four gold stars emblazoned on the visor of his cap, looking out over the multitude with the air of a conqueror.

'Good,' Jeannot said. 'Then we can start the rosary.' He looked at me. 'Paul, a moment?'

Taking my arm, he walked me past the microphones until we were out of earshot of the others. He put his hands on my shoulders and looked up at me. Those extraordinary eyes brimmed with tears. 'Do you remember Toumalie, Paul? The day you found me and brought me here?'

'Yes, of course.'

'Do you regret it?'

'No, *Petit*. Of course not.'

'I love you,' he said. 'I always will.'

I, myself, was in tears.

'Now,' he said. 'Let us begin.'

He stepped up on to a small platform, erected so that he could be seen over the tops of the assembled microphones. He looked out on the immense crowd and raised his arms in a gesture of peace. As he did, hundreds of posters bearing his picture were hoisted aloft. Cheers and cries of 'Jeannot! Jeannot!' echoed across the Place Notre Dame. I looked back at General Macandal. He stood, statue still, staring up at the sky, as if to ignore the sight before his eyes.

Again, Jeannot raised his arms.

'Rosaries! Do we have our rosaries?'

Thousands of hands held up sets of rosary beads. Tiny candles, flickering feebly in the sunlight, were also held aloft. Jeannot gestured for silence.

With this recitation of the rosary
We ask our mother Mary
To intercede for us
To ask her son, Jesus Christ,
To lead us to the freedom that was promised us.

We ask God's help.
Without it, we will fail.
Let us pray.

Making the sign of the cross, Jeannot began to recite the rosary. As his voice ended the first verse of the Ave Maria, he was answered by a vast mumble from thousands of throats. I watched him, a small, frail figure wearing the anonymous, cheap cotton clothing of the poor, with, behind him, like a frieze of pomp and circumstance, the elegant figures of Lambert and Caroline, the gold-braided officers, the purple-robed Bishop, the clergy in their starched white surplices and red soutanes. And, in the centre of the group, sweating under the morning sun, the imposing grizzled head of the senator who, from this day on, would, as premier, represent all of these powers.

Jeannot intoned the Aves. The multitude responded. The rosary is the most mechanical of devotions, repetitious, familiar, a prayer of rote. But that morning I heard it as I had never heard it before, not as a prayer but as a muttering chant, the words repeated over and over like a slogan. Among the people grouped on the steps around me, only the young priests and nuns gave out the responses. Beside me, Caroline Lambert plucked at a thread on her silk handbag, bored and impatient as a child in church. General Macandal and his officers, the Bishop and senior clergy, stood silent, staring out at the chanting multitude as though they faced an angry mob.

I did not pray. To me, that morning, the words of the rosary were a repetitious thunder of voices imploring a blue and empty sky. Who could believe that in those cold heavens, Christ's mother listened to their plea?

Jeannot reached the final decade. At the last response he raised his hand to his forehead, and made the sign of the cross. The multitude followed suit. There was a moment of silence, broken only by the eerie hum of the waiting loudspeakers. Behind Jeannot, white against the blue sky, their arms outstretched in poses of piety, I saw the huge statues of a dying Christ, a blessed Virgin, a stern Saint Peter. And, again, Jeannot's voice, quiet, incantatory, that voice like no other, crept out into the great square.

Brothers and Sisters,
My hour is past.
My day is done.
When you can no longer see me,
When you can no longer find me,
I will be with you.
I will be with you
As will those who have died from soldiers' bullets,
Who lie in ditches,
Their bodies rotting,
Their minds stilled.
They are not dead.
They live on in you.
They wait
As I wait
For you to change our lives.
But, you ask me
Who will be our leader?
The dead are our leaders.
You and only you
With the help of God
And the memory of the dead
Can bring about our freedom.
It will not happen in a day
Or in a year.
It will not happen in a riot
Or in a parliament of fools.
It will happen when you
No longer ask

For a Messiah.
You are the Messiah.
As for me
I am nothing
I came from nothing.
Today I go back
To those from whom I came,
The poor, the silent, the unknown.
From today on
We wait for you.
As the dead wait for you.
To bring us freedom.
Brothers and Sisters,
You are the anointed ones.
With God's help
You will not fail.

He bowed his head. The loudspeakers hummed in eerie
tension. Then, abruptly leaving the podium, he walked down
the steps and went towards the great multitude, his arms outstretched as if to embrace them. Suddenly, sticks beat on
sticks, drums pounded, tin cans rattled, voices chorused,
'Jeannot! Jeannot!' Heads bobbed up and down. People
rushed forward, embracing him, passing him on from one
group to another, as he went deeper and deeper into the mass
of bodies. In less than a minute I could no longer see him.
Lambert's dark-suited thugs, who had hung back, now
plunged into the crowd trying desperately to locate him. But
the mass of people, like a great wave, pushed them aside.

I saw Lambert signal to his soldiers who quickly formed a
ring around Caroline as though expecting her to be attacked.
But the vast, chanting, drumming throng ignored the lines of
dignitaries massed on the cathedral steps. The huge square
exploded into sound and movement as, the prayers ended, a
wild celebration began. After a moment, the dignitaries

turned to each other, confused. General Macandal signalled to the Bishop and both went back into the church. The elite and their wives exchanged hasty farewells and hurried to their limousines. The young nuns and priests rushed down into the square, joining the celebration.

Crossing the now empty steps, coming towards me, I saw the familiar bulk of Noël Destouts in his frayed soutane and red Cuban sandals.

'Paul, did you know about this?'

'No.'

Below us, a mass of swirling bodies, four thousand bobbing heads, a deafening, joyous, carnival din.

'*Mesiah*,' Noël said.

ELEVEN

I HAVE AN EXCELLENT MEMORY,' Colonel Lambert said. ' "When you can no longer see me, when you can no longer find me, I will be with you." Those were his exact words. Do you agree, Father?'

I said I did.

'Accusations that he has been killed by police or army agents are, I can assure you, totally false. In my view, the sentence I have just quoted to you means that he didn't flee abroad, that he is somewhere on this island, hiding like a lizard under a rock, and by this tactic encouraging the civil unrest and rioting of the past two months. More deaths, is that what he wants?'

'I've told you, I don't know what he wants.'

'Second point. Foreign businesses are pulling out of Ganae to a far greater extent than is generally known. And when factories close here, they won't open again. Result: the misery of the common people will be greater than ever before. Is that what he wants?'

'There's no point in your telling me all this,' I said. 'I am not in touch with him.'

'I don't believe you, Father. I'm sure you mean well. You're a good man, everyone says so. I'm going to be honest with you. General Macandal wants to take a stronger line with dissenters and those clergy who continue to promote civil unrest. That will mean more interrogations and detentions. But before that happens I wanted to invite you here to see if there is any way we can convince your friend that we're willing to discuss further political compromise if it will help to end this crisis.'

We were sitting in one of the living rooms in Lambert's mansion, which was rumoured to be the largest private house in Ganae. One wall of the room was glass, with a view of a swimming pool, designed to give the impression that it was a Roman bath. As we talked, Caroline Lambert swam slowly, gracefully, up and down the pool. Embarrassed, I realised that I had not stopped watching her.

I said to Lambert, 'You know that I am not in touch with him. You have had me followed day and night. My correspondence has been opened and I believe my telephone calls are being monitored. My friend Pelardy is in jail, held for the past three months without charge. In the slums of the cities and in villages and towns throughout the country innocent people have been beaten and shot to stifle their protests against the regime which you have put in place. If I knew where Jeannot was, I wouldn't advise him to meet you. It would put his life in danger.'

'That's not true,' Lambert said. 'I'll ignore your accusations and exaggerations. If Father Cantave can be persuaded to come forward, then you can be certain no one would dare to harm him. The whole world is curious as to his fate. He knows very well that he would be safe.'

At that point, Caroline Lambert climbed out of the swimming pool. A maid was waiting with a large white bath wrap, and a parasol which she held over Caroline's head. The ladies of the mulatto elite fear the sun: for them it is the colour of darkness. Caroline, followed by her servant, walked towards us along the edge of the pool and, seeing me in the living room, theatrically mimed surprise then slid open the glass door and came inside.

'Father Michel, what a pleasure! How are you? Excuse me, I'm wet and horrid, I must go and change. But, how nice to see you. Alain, you must arrange that Father Michel come to dinner soon. Remember our journey on the mules, Father? What an adventure that was.'

She went on through the suite of huge rooms and waved to me just before I lost sight of her. It was the last time I spoke to Caroline Lambert. Now, I look back to my foolish passion for her as yet another mockery of my wasted life. I did see her once again, a few years later, at a reception that I attended to welcome a new minister of education. While I was being introduced to the minister in my capacity as principal of the Collège St Jean, Caroline Lambert came up to us. She wore a golden evening dress and looked more beautiful than ever. My heart jumped. She greeted the minister warmly but when she was introduced to me, she smiled, mouthed the polite greeting one makes to a stranger, then walked on.

Her husband did not forget me. Some weeks after our meeting in his house, I was taken from the college residence in the middle of the night and interrogated in Fort Noël. The questions were no different from those that had been asked before. Where was Jeannot? Who had I seen last month when I went to Jamaica to visit our Provincial? The manner, however, was different. I was punched, kicked and called a liar, held in Fort Noël for three days and released only when, through our Order, my plight was communicated to Rome and Cardinal Innocenti. Apologies were offered to the Provincial and to the papal nuncio, but not to me.

A few days after my release from Fort Noël, the nuncio handed me a letter from Cardinal Innocenti which had been sent by diplomatic pouch. It was marked 'confidential' and sealed with a papal seal. In it, the Cardinal expressed his regret for what had happened to me and asked if I had any news of Jeannot. He also said he was anxious to have my impressions of the current state of affairs in Ganae. Any information I could give him would, he reassured me, remain confidential.

I was grateful for his efforts in securing my release and in my report I tried to summarise my own impressions and conjectures. I told him that 'All searches, killings, beatings and other intimidation of Father Cantave's followers among the poor have failed to quench their faith in his eventual return, and so the government seems to have decided that its wisest course of action is to pretend that the battle is won. Father Cantave's name is never mentioned by the government-controlled media. If questioned about his return, civilian and army leaders pretend indifference. Raymond, the premier, recently told *Le Monde* that "Cantave is now irrelevant. Ganae has moved on to a new stage of democracy." I should also mention a statement made by Archbishop Pellerat to a group of visiting American bishops, which may not have come to the attention of Your Eminence. He was quoted as saying, "The ideas of social revolt promulgated by Father Cantave have been repudiated by the poor. They have had enough of the rioting and killings that his teachings inspired. In addition, his followers among the clergy, those priests and nuns who advocated radical social change, have been left without leadership."

'Your Eminence, the truth of the matter seems to be that Father Cantave's ideas have not been repudiated but, indeed, have in some way been strengthened by his mysterious absence. The poor, more than ever, consider him a sort of Messiah and await his eventual return.

'To answer your primary question I have no news at all of Father Cantave, nor do I expect to have any. He did not confide in me before his disappearance. In our last days together he told me that people must not rely on one leader. They must learn to make the revolution themselves. When I asked him how they could do that, he answered, "Christ was a leader who did not lead." It is possible therefore that, in some way, he hopes to emulate Our Lord by passing into legend. I do not expect to see him again.'

A month after I sent this report I received a reply from Cardinal Innocenti thanking me for my 'interesting and informative letter.' He made no comment on its contents and hoped that I would call on him, if ever I revisited Rome.

TWELVE

IT IS NOW TEN YEARS since that day when Jeannot seemed to disappear from this earth. There has been no revolution but, to the dismay of the elite and the Army, an ungovernable rage and resentment consumes the daily lives of the poor. In the slums of La Rotonde and Doumergueville and in the wretched villages of Cap Nord and Mele, candles are lit daily to Jeannot's memory. Small, homemade shrines may be seen at country crossroads and on the barren hillsides of Cap Gauche, Papanos and Pondicher. The shrines are religious, with a crucifix at their head, as though to ward off the vampires of the regime. Most contain crude images of Jeannot, but there is also an oleograph or statue of the Virgin Mary. Because of this intermingling of religious iconography with Jeannot's image, even the brutal soldiers of the new special battalions have not dared to desecrate or destroy these shrines. And so they have stood for years, tended with flowers, restored after storms. Women kneel before them, on their long journeys from village to city. Workers, passing them on their way to the fields, make the sign of the cross and bow their heads.

In parliament, the *noirs* have used Jeannot's memory to

force the *mulâtres* to share legislative power. Because of this, *noirs* now occupy most of the ministerial posts and are installed in the highest positions in the Army and police. But nothing has changed. The system is, as always, totally corrupt. The poor are its victims.

In the past ten years there have been many rumours and false sightings. Some of the people have always believed that Jeannot was murdered by Macandal's soldiers: others say that he is alive and will return to lead an armed revolt. His name is never mentioned among the elite but the mystery of his disappearance sits under the arrogance and privilege of their lives, like a dangerous earthquake fault.

At the beginning of this account, I wrote that I want to record the hidden event, the story never told. I do not know who will read these pages. I have asked myself: Is it my duty to remain silent? Or is it my duty to tell?

A year after Jeannot's disappearance, Father Bourque retired and I became Principal of the Collège St Jean. One morning when I was in my office, preparing class rosters, our doorman told me that there was a woman waiting to speak to me at the front entrance.

'Who is she?'

'She will not say, sir. She is from the country. They are very ignorant people in that place. I know it, sir. It's called Toumalie.'

Toumalie. I looked up from my papers. 'Put her in the visitor's parlour. I'll come down.'

But when I reached the ground-floor parlour the doorman came up to me. 'I'm sorry, sir, but the woman will not come in.'

I went outside. A tall woman was standing near the front door. She was one of those who make the long journey each day from distant villages to the central market at Port Riche. She had lowered her market bundles to the ground and stood beside them, nervous, looking as if she might bolt.

I went up to her. 'Good morning. I am Father Michel. Can I help you?'

She stared at me for a moment, then with a sudden shy smile reached into the red-and-yellow bandanna that covered her head and took out an object which she handed to me. It was a pocket watch, with a gold case that closed over the dial. My hand trembled as I snapped open the case and saw the initials I had ordered engraved on its inside. J.P.C. I shut the case. The woman was lifting her bundles from the ground.

'Wait. Who gave you this?'

She smiled, balanced the huge bundles on her head and, erect and stately, walked off towards the college gates. I hurried after her.

'Please? Tell me who gave you this. And why did you bring it here?'

'I am sorry,' she said, and kept on walking.

'You are from Toumalie?'

'Yes.'

'Please tell me. Who?'

'He just ask me to bring it,' she said, quickening her pace as we passed through the gates. 'Because I come to Port Riche, two times each week.'

'Who asked you?'

'Frédéric.'

'Frédéric who?'

'Please, *Mon Pe*. Let me go now.'

She hurried off down the street.

I left the car in Melun. It was twenty-one years since I had been in Toumalie but there was still no road over which a car could safely travel. I set off on muleback in early afternoon, knowing there would be no bed for me that night if I did not sleep at the house of the local priest. And, of course, I could not do that. When I came into the village, a little after four o'clock, I saw some women washing clothes in a stream at the side of the road. Children played and splashed in the water. Further upstream a man squatted in the shallows while his wife scrubbed his back. I rode up to this couple and asked if they could tell me where to find Frédéric.

A priest, even a *blanc* priest, is not a dangerous person in a place like Toumalie. 'Frédéric, there are two Frédérics,' the man said. 'Young Frédéric, you want?'

'How old is he?'

'I don't know. A boy.'

'No,' I said. 'The other one.'

The man stood up, dripping, and shook himself like a dog. 'They're on the hill,' he said. He pointed. 'See that shack up there? It's not that one. Next one up is Frédéric's.'

I thanked him and went on. As the mule picked its way along the narrow rocky path I wondered if this was the same path down which I had carried Jeannot twenty-one years ago. When I passed the first shack, two small children ran out and seeing me, a stranger, ran back in again. The second shack was larger and had recently been reroofed with tin. There was a ramshackle porch and in front of it a heap of cooking stones, a sign that the shack had no kitchen. Again, children ran out, three girls and a little boy. But these children, seeing me, did not run away. They stood and stared as I threw the mule's reins over its neck and climbed down, stiff and aching. Somewhere in the distance a cock crowed. I looked up at the hillside behind the house and saw tiny terraced fields fenced in by rocks to keep the soil from slipping down the mountainside. The children watched me and the smallest, the boy, ran over to a little shed behind the main shack.

'Papa,' he called.

The shed door opened, loose on creaking hinges, and a man stepped out. He was small and frail, his hair like steel wool, tight-knitted to his skull. As he came towards me I felt a sudden shock. I had never seen him before but I knew him. I held out the watch. He looked at it, then looked at me angrily. 'She told you my name?'

'Frédéric?'

He nodded. He pointed to the porch. 'The sun is still hot,' he said. 'Let's go in.'

We walked up on to the porch and sat on the rickety chairs. He turned to the children, who were watching. 'Go inside.'

Obedient, they filed past us into the shack. The screen door banged shut.

'You look like him,' I said. 'I would have known you. Where are your cousins? Is your aunt still alive?'

'She's dead. My cousins have all left Toumalie. Some work in a factory in Papanos, the rest are labourers in a mill in Pondicher. I did not want to leave. So I try to work this farm.'

He leaned back in his rickety chair and in a familiar gesture put his hand up, his fingers covering his eyes. I could have been watching Jeannot.

'You should not have come here,' he said. 'Your coming is dangerous for us.'

'No one knows I am here. And I will tell no one.'

'But what if they find out? Many times in the past they have come here, police and soldiers, asking, looking everywhere, telling us they will beat us. They know my name is Cantave. I tell them always the same thing, that you took him from us when he was a child. I told them that he never came back to see us, not once. All true, as you know. But now, if they find out you have come, they will say I lied to them.'

'They will not know. I promise you.'

'How can you promise that? Those children you saw just now, they are mine and they are dear to me. I put them in danger because of him. I didn't want him to come back. He never helped us. We did not exist for him. But when he came, alone, after all those years, I said to myself, "I mustn't do as he did." So I took him in.'

'Where is he?'

'He is dead. He died last winter. There is a fever, I don't know the name. There are no doctors here. My children caught this fever but they are young and strong. He caught it from them but he was—you know—always sick and weak. He sweated and fought it, but the fever did not break for him. On the third night, he died.'

I looked at the watch that I held in my hand. From the moment the woman gave it to me I had known it was a knell. I opened the gold case and saw again his initials. J.P.C.

'Why did you send me this? Did he ask you to?'

Frédéric shook his head. 'No. He didn't think he would die. But his time had come. I sent it to you because it is yours, not mine. As he was yours. You took him away, you made him what he was. I didn't like what he was. How many hundreds have died because of his preachings? How many more would die tomorrow if they thought it would bring him back?'

'Where is he buried?'

He hesitated, then said, 'All right, I will tell you. He is up there on the hill. I buried him myself. I told no one. And I ask you, Father. Tell no one. If you do, people will come here to pray and make trouble. They may even want to take him from the grave. And then the soldiers will come and beat me and put me in prison. My family will suffer. And for what?'

I stood up. Grief had come upon me like a panic. I wanted to weep, to run outside.

I said, 'I must get back to Melun before night. May I see the grave?'

'Yes. Come.'

Behind the ramshackle house, a footpath led up through the meagre fields. He walked ahead, not looking back. He said, 'It's good that you visit the grave. You can say the prayers. I prayed there myself when I put him down, but I'm not a priest.'

On a muddy slope, which tilted so steeply that it could not be farmed, he stopped and pointed to the ground. I saw no

sign of a grave. Leaves and mud covered the place he indicated. 'I did it at night,' he said. 'The children don't know
where it is. Not even my wife knows. Of course, I could not
put up a cross. You can see for yourself. No one would know
that this ground has been touched.'

He paused, then said, 'I'll leave you to your prayers. You
can find your own way down. Goodbye. And please. Don't
come again.'

'I won't. Thank you.'

He shook his head angrily, dismissing my thanks. Turning,
he went back down the narrow path.

And then I was alone with Jeannot, alone for the last time. I
looked at the ground, anonymous as the unmarked graves of
peasants who had died a hundred years ago. Jeannot, his incantatory voice for ever silent, Jeannot who had passed into
legend. If only he *were* the Messiah, if only the gravestone
could be rolled back. But I stood on this earth and he lay
beneath it, his frail body returning, ashes to ashes, dust to
dust.

I knelt down by the unmarked grave but not to pray. I
touched the muddied earth in a useless caress as though,
somehow, he would know that I had come here. I wept but
my tears could not help him. There is no other life.

The little boy, Frédéric's youngest child, stood by the mule as
I came back down into the yard. He was trying to feed it a
handful of grass. He looked up at me. 'Take me for a ride,
Mon Pe?'

I put him on the mule's back and walked the mule around
the yard. His sisters watched us from the window but did not
come out.

When I went to lift him off, he cried. 'More! More! Take
me down the hill.'

'No, *Petit*. Stay here.'